MY BEARD WAS A YULETIDE SERIAL KILLER

A YULETIDE HORROR

BY
DALE M. CHATWIN

A Kvasir's Blood Publication ©

Kvasir's blood was mingled with honey, thence was made the mead of poetry

This is a work of fiction. Names, characters, businesses, places, events, locales, and incidents are either the products of the author's imagination or used in a fictitious manner. Any resemblance to actual persons, living or dead, or actual events is purely coincidental.

Printed by Amazon Kindle Direct Publishing for Kvasir's Blood Publications

ISBN: 9798358536678

Cover Design and Rear Cover Badge by Nikki Rennie-Smith ©2022

Edited by Alice Bezant

Author Photograph by Kate Ryan

kvasirsbloodpublications@gmail.com

ONE

No one can really pinpoint the exact moment they discover that their beard is a serial killer. Leif Fabian can.

It was a moment he would never forget, though there have been plenty of times when he wished upon a star that he could. Who could blame him? The moment was just so utterly absurd, and like an iron of white heat it had been branded on the flabby mass of thoughts inside his head for all eternity.

As he lay in the cast iron cauldron that was more bathtub than witch's pot, surrounded by the warm vapour of evaporating alcohol, and the warmer liquid enveloping his body, Leif thought back to that moment and all the other moments that had led him to this point. The pungent aromas of Christmas spices slithered up his nostrils and in this liquid cocoon he felt a metamorphosis creeping upon him.

Don't worry buddy you deserve this, said the voice he had become unwillingly familiar with during the build up to Christmas.

Leif smiled at something, but the alcohol was flushing through his bloodstream at a million miles an hour and his head tumbled through a vortex of brainy slush and incoherence.

That something smiled back.

As the cauldron grew warmer, Leif thought about the day it all started.

It was a cursed day. It was the day that kicked off. The unending horror. The horror with a hairy disposition.

Two

It begins like every other Christmas story that has never happened, with a storm and a dead body.

At midnight on the first day of December, the coastal town of Mevagissey in Cornwall fell victim to a savage snowstorm that devastated the first official day of the Christmas season. Blizzards of frosty white blew the boats anchored in the harbour. They swayed like swaggering drunkards upon the dark water. What would usually be a beautiful moonlit spectacle in the summer was now a confused and frightening scenario of crashing waves and thick falling snow, with winds that brought chaos and minor destruction.

No-one was brave enough or foolish enough to be wandering the streets during that terrible storm. If they had been they would have seen the eldritch flashes of red and green light behind the clouds and would have been hard pressed to figure out what exactly was causing that phenomenon

When daylight came the population of Mevagissey awoke to the illustrious sight of sparkling snow. The storm had dissipated and left behind a jewel that signified the beginning of Christmas anticipation. It was a day that reminded folk of how Christmas should really look, like it is in films and books created to spread festive cheer. Houses were beginning to be adorned with Yuletide decorations, and all memory of the storm was being washed away by the harbours in their minds. The harbour master in Mevagissey however could not wash away the simple fact that the harbour had to be closed due to the weather. This sent shockwaves of vague disappointment through the local boating community. It was only a fleeting disappointment because Christmas was around the corner and who could stay disappointed during this festive time? On normal occasions the harbour wouldn't close if there had been fair warning of the storm, but because of its abruptness the harbour master's hand was forced. The Inner Harbour and the boats within were unharmed, which was a testament to how the Victorians designed its shape. The Outer Harbour suffered a severe beating from the storm, resulting in a project of restoration that would take at least a year to complete.

Despite all the chaos the spirit of Christmas was now safe to enter the halls of the Cornish consciousness. On the evening of the first day of December the folk of Mevagissey gathered at the harbour to watch the Christmas lights being turned on. It was a spectacular sight to behold and boats were decorated with fairy lights: when switched on they looked like ships from the bygone days of wonder. In the harbour was an illuminated sea creature designed to look like it was coming out of the water, and all along the harbour were the shapes of lit up Christmas trees and bells and angels. People drank mulled wine, mulled cider, munching on bags of roasted chestnuts and German sausage, laughing with one another and joining in that festive community spirit that happens like a spark of happiness once a year at Christmas. Through large speakers attached to buildings the familiar songs played, the ones that had been tucked away all year round to be brought out when the seasonal celebrations began. The memory of the storm was all but distant in the minds of the locals, and they looked towards the future and concentrated on the good will of all men and women. Christmastime in Mevagissey was a special time, and when Leif Fabian walked around the narrow streets seeing the oodles of good cheer all around him, he was thankful to be a part of that wonderful community. He received many compliments about his beard that evening - especially from the local women – and even though he had undergone an upsetting experience the night before he smiled and thanked them and indulged in the festivities and mulled wine. He was determined not to wallow in his own mulled self-loathing.

Then the good cheer slipped into dead seriousness when the first body was found.

The second day of December opened with a scream that would have woken the dead if the dead were accustomed to awakening. It happened at seven-thirty in the morning, as the first limbs of pale daylight were stretching across the autumn sky in a desperate bid to radiate the land in warmth, but warmth was a distant memory now, and more snow started to fall. The sun was an impotent disc hanging in a barren sky of pregnant clouds. A man in his early seventies was out walking his Scottish terrier along the controversially named Hitler's Walk. It was a path just off Polkirt Hill that ran down a bank of grass and bushes and overlooked the English Channel and the village. The view from its highest point was said to be the best in the town. Hitler's Walk was named from an urban legend about a woman who claimed to have seen the ghost of Adolf Hitler roaming the park. He was then seen staring out across the English Channel on Christmas Eve the year nineteen sixty-nine. She had said his eyes were full of sorrow as he dreamed of his lost Third Reich. The tale was of course the preposterous ramblings of a known spinster who was whacked out on acid and as the years droned on the quirky name stuck to the pathway like the ectoplasm of that non-existent Nazi ghost. The path itself had caused quite a stir over the years for having such a blacklisted name. Local protest groups had tried to get the name changed over the years. They had failed at every turn.

The little terrier was black and stood out against the ivory snow. It trotted ahead of the man leaving little paw prints in the pristine white blanket of path.

'Dixie, don't get too far ahead,' the man called out to the terrier. It paid him no heed and trotted further down the path until it stopped in front of a lamppost and started yapping. The man couldn't see any other dogs around.

'Come back girl,' he called out again and this time whistled.

Dixie did not come to him. She only kept yapping.

The snow was falling in dense flakes at this point and the man pulled his thick coat around him tighter. He took careful steps along the path towards Dixie and her incessant yapping concerned him greatly. She must have found something. The first thing that caught his eye was red against the stark white snow. It was the kind of red that could make a man go blind with madness.

He didn't scream until he saw the contorted corpse over an angel shaped pool of crimson.

THREE

For Leif Fabian the snowstorm meant slow business at the aquarium. The whole winter period was slow anyway and when Jack Frost came knocking people started hiding. He woke on the first day of December wondering why his beard looked peculiarly more full than it had the day before. In the bathroom mirror he stroked the mass of brown hairs growing around the bottom half of his face and scrunched his forehead with curiosity.

Must be all that testosterone, he thought and laughed to himself. He had started growing his beard four months ago, much to the dislike of his now estranged girlfriend Phoebe Marley. She had dumped him the night before telling him it was not a breakup but merely a separation of souls free to explore themselves and their wants in order to discover whether they really are supposed to be together. She said that they would eventually be drawn back to one another when the time was right. If the time was ever right. But he knew the real reason why. Leif tried arguing the point in the beginning, but Phoebe just pushed herself away until she concluded that it would be best that they don't keep in contact until *she* felt the time was right. Phoebe hated beards. She always heckled him to shave it off saying it was dirty and had read in an article on the Internet that shit particles get trapped in the follicles making them the most unclean things on the planet. He laughed at the ridiculousness of that statement and mocked her for believing in fake news, which just exasperated her mood. It was not however the reason for this "separation of souls."

He was impressed with how much it had grown in the four-month period since that shadow of stubble appeared one morning and he decided to keep it growing. He was even more impressed with how much it had grown overnight.

Leif's house was on Cliff Road amongst a large cluster of houses perched atop a hill. All of them overlooked the harbour. When he left his house on that first day of December he was greeted by vast whiteness. He breathed in the crisp Christmassy air and smiled. He had only lived in Mevagissey for two years and in that time had never seen such a sight as the one he looked at that day. He made his way to work at the aquarium and just as he predicted no one visited. It was a dead day. In the evening he attended the ceremony of turning on the Christmas lights and felt more positive about the future. It was only a temporary feeling.

The second day of December was a Saturday, and though there was no storm the snow fell with dense determination. Leif decided to keep the aquarium closed. He was the manager and owner after all and had that authority. He had bought the aquarium off the St Austell council using inheritance money left to him when his father passed away. Since buying it he transformed the building into a far more popular attraction than it had been and turned it into a place of education and aquatic curiosity.

It wasn't just the weather that deterred him from going into work. It was the dreams too. He had awoken that day from a nightmare where he was swallowed by a horse, spending an eternity inside its stomach being digested deliberately across the aeons, before waking in a cold greasy sweat. The dream played on his mind for the rest of the day because he recognized the horse. It was a Fjord horse he wished he could have kept buried, but skeletons of the past have a terrible habit of finding their way back to the surface.

Leif needed breakfast he needed something cooked with lots of meat so he decided to head to his local pub, The Fountain Inn, which was located on Cliff Street near where he lived. It was considered the oldest pub in town and dated back to the fifteenth century. Its low ceilings were painted white, with black beams hanging low, still retaining that smuggler's den décor to give the interior a more authentic appearance. It looked like the kind of place that smugglers and pirates would still frequent, where whispered words, sea shanties, suspicious glances, would fill the hazy atmosphere.

Leif wove his way through the narrow pathless streets, out of view of the harbour and the commotion that was happening on the other side on Hitler's Walk.

Even on a cold autumn mid-morning the close-knit network of ivy that covered the front of the pub was still as resplendent as ever, even without the flowers that wouldn't bloom until late in the New Year. It was Swedish ivy meaning it lasted all year round and was planted by the pub's owner, Glenda Cartwright. Glenda was a familiar acquaintance of Leif's and his regular visits to the pub meant they often engaged in discussions about local history. She was one of his mentors in the ways of Mevagissey living.

That day the pub was quiet and Glenda was nowhere to be seen. A sullen atmosphere lay heavy inside like fog smothering a moor. Being a six-foot-four-inch tall gentleman, he felt like a vertically impaired monster in The Fountain Inn having to stoop to ensure his head did not fall victim to those wicked wooden beams.

Old Herbert Hunkin was perched on his usual stool at the bar sipping a pint of St Austell ale in his own tankard, and in his left hand he twirled his pipe between his fingers. He was known for smoking his tobacco in an old clay pipe whose nozzle had been carved into the shape of a pilchard head, the fish he and his ancestors used to cultivate from the oceanic farms off the coast of Cornwall. Herbert was a lonely man in his seventies and a retired Fishman from the days when Mevagissey was still the central point of Britain's fishing industry. These days he used his old fishing boat to take tourists out on a thirty-minute cruise along the coast. His grey hair was like wisps of smoke, with a bristly moustache layering his top lip that had a habit of catching the froth every time he took a sip.

Solitary candles were laid on the wooden tables around the pub, their flames flickering from the occasional breeze that blew in through miscellaneous crevasses in the ancient brickwork.

On that day Herbert had tears in his eyes.

Leif took a seat next to the sorrowful man and ordered a coffee from the barman.

'What's wrong Herbert?' asked Leif.

'Glenda's dead,' said Herbert and a fresh flood of tears poured from his eyes.

'Dead? How?' Leif's mouth was agape and his face was flushed red as the news seeped into his thoughts.

'Murdered by some god-awful scum. Happened early this morning. Her body was on the steep bank of grass at the highest point of Hitler's Walk and must have been used to make a snow angel first. It looked like her blood had been drained into the angel where it all froze up like some macabre ice pop and her pale body was stood up at the head of it. The redness of the blood almost blinded me. It looked like it was glowing against the snow, throbbing with some horrid light that shouldn't exist. Her arms and hands were all twisted to look like frozen water or something inhuman. There were even icicles of frozen blood hanging from her fingertips. It looked like they had been frozen while pouring into the pool. She looked like a fountain statue, a dead angel. It was horrific and bizarre. I can't explain it all, Leif, lest I go mad. I'll never sleep soundly again. I'll never make snow angels again and if my grandchildren ever make them in my presence, I might scream myself to death. The police can't fathom how she would have frozen up like that. The way she was positioned, how solid the blood was… it would have to have happened within minutes. It was damn cold last night, but not that cold.'

'Jesus, Herbert how do you know all this?'

'I found the body. In all my years living in this village I have never seen anything like it. You hear of this kind of stuff happening somewhere like America not in a place like Mevagissey. It's the stuff of films and trashy novels or those horrible video games the kids play, not real life. Poor Glenda. I'll have nightmares about that for the rest of my short life. The grotesque pain she must have suffered. Her eyes were open too, Leif, and she looked like she was gazing out over village towards where you live. Looking with a dead stare.'

Leif wept with Herbert and ordered a whisky for them both. They spent the rest of the day drinking and reminiscing about Glenda. At six o'clock in the evening Leif's best friend Dexter Kloppers entered the pub and more drinking ensued. By the night-time the pub was packed full of local patrons who all loved Glenda. They sang and cried and shared memories. It was the spirit of community of close-knit kith and kin coming together in a time of turmoil and overcoming the sadness by celebrating the life of those whose time has come.

The next body would not be found until a week later, on the ninth day of December.

Four

Dreams of hair and gnawing fangs plagued his nights. Images of snowflakes made of chomping teeth and teams of horses champing at his feet and stamping on his eyeballs, turning them into cranberry jelly, woke him in cold shuddering fits. Sweat dripped like leaking cracks in cave walls. He dreamed of Glenda and he saw his own beard committing the murder. Thick strands of his facial forest reached out with pernicious purpose and wrapped around her body in hairy coils, tightening with every breath she took, constricting her life force and snuffing her soul out of existence. Bewilderment infected his mind when he tried to fathom as to why he was having these villainous visions.

It was on low days when Leif liked to go out into the whimsical waters on his boat, the *Saffron Siren*. Leif had named the boat when he bought it two years ago upon moving to Mevagissey. It was an ex-fishing boat with a mystical saffron paint job that seduced him into purchasing it and, like a siren, he suspected it would one day wreck him on the craggy coast of

Cornwall where he would drown in his own terrible destiny. It was a morbid thought to possess, but the image it evoked seemed somewhat epic and apocalyptic. The main purpose of purchasing the boat was so he could catch marine life from the local waters to display at the aquarium, but he also loved to head out and mediate among the waves. The waves were like wrinkles on the furrowed brow of an elderly person, each ripple telling a tale of long ago on the ocean, with every licking wave mimicking a tongue of secrets, teasing with their nautical mischief and a moistened touch of deceit.

On the third day of December when the news of Glenda's grisly demise had spread around the village. Leif decided to take the Saffron Siren out for an evening. He weighed anchor across from Chapel Point that was known as "The Famous House" because it was featured in a well-known Daphne du Maurier novel. Leif had read the book when he first moved to Mevagissey and discovered the house's existence. Two days after the storm the harbour reopened after receiving word that there would be no more savage squalls. The snow continued to fall though and this did not bother Leif. He was raised in Norway and snow was an old friend of his.

The water was calm during that night and the boat rocked gently, almost lulling Leif into a slumber, the blinking of the lighthouse nurturing him like a comforting nightlight. His beard was beginning to feel irritable: it itched, and when he scratched it he did it with such ferocity that flakes of dead white skin cascaded onto his coat, instantly blending in with the flakes of live white snow. The option to shave it was off the table. He was impressed with how much it had grown and on his occasional trips into more populated areas he received much praise for his beard. Even at thirty-five years old he marvelled at how there was not one single streak of grey lurking in those follicles. His long shaggy brown hair was a different story: bits of grey peppered the strands and the follicular garnish was thinning into what would eventually be baldness. Most of the time he wore a ribbed burgundy woolly hat to cover this revelation. His breath exhaled in plumes of steam against the frosty air. Eventually he succumbed to sleep's insistent tug and he slipped into another nightmarish world. This time, he saw stars filled with blood and flesh being cut like cookie dough. The smells of sweet baked goods stirred his hunger, but the horrific images made him squeamish.

When he woke Leif was dithering and covered in snow. He stood up quickly, moved around to warm his body, and then started the boat for home.

The mood in Mevagissey was cold. The local police department had made no progress in their investigation, even with the help of detectives from Plymouth. There was a serious lack of clues at the crime scene and all their leads had gone cold; like everything else, and the tendrils of the snowstorm had found its way into the case, freezing into icy stillness. Those who suffered from a more superstitious disposition worried that the village was going to be buried in the snow and be suffocated in a cold blanket of sin.

The third day of December was a Sunday, and whilst Leif had been on his boat contemplating the death of his friend, the Church of St Peter experienced a full congregation for evening mass. To many of the residents it seemed the Devil had paid a visit to Mevagissey and now they needed to plead to God's merciful side.

The next morning the snow eased up enough for the sun to come out and radiate the sky, but its warmth could not penetrate the frosty firmament.

The moods of the townsfolk picked up slightly and some allowed themselves to settle into the seasonal cheer of Christmas. Leif looked out over the harbour. The tide was out, a thick blanket of snow covered the sand, and the boats looked like they were locked in the arctic tundra. In the snow he saw the tiny prints of bird feet tracing hither and thither all over the whiteness. Leif remembered summer at low tide when the harbour would be laden with green seaweed. To him it had looked like some obnoxious and inconsiderate giant had sneezed upon the harbour and smeared its grotesque snot everywhere in a final act of spite. The image always made him chuckle.

Across the way he saw that Hitler's walk was no longer cordoned off by the police and he could make out the shapes of children playing and building snowmen, ignorant of the horror that had occurred up there.

In the mirror of his bathroom Leif once again noticed a change in his beard and still it grew at a rate that seemed impossible. When he stroked that thick mass of hair it felt coarse and dry. It felt old. He wanted to trim it to a healthier length, but work was beckoning him.

The beard would have to wait.

Five

The aquarium was the old lifeboat station at the bottom of Polkirt Hill on the edge of the harbour. It was painted in an aesthetically pleasing sky blue with attractive typography on the side. Inside there were huge tanks that displayed different forms of marine life caught from the waters outside the harbour. It was a pleasant job for Leif and it gave him the chance to study the various fish and crustaceans that cruised in the local briny waters.

During his feeding of those aquatic critters his beard began to furiously itch and while he satisfied it with a more furious scratch an image flashed in his mind's eye of a tank of blood, and a creepy cadaver in the water being nibbled away by the fish. The image sickened him and he wondered why such a horrible thought would appear so suddenly and so randomly.

'Have you been dying your beard?' a deep Cornish voice boomed through the front door. Leif leaped out of his skin. He turned and saw Bruce Huxley, the harbour master, and one of Leif's closest friends, standing in the doorway.

Before Leif moved to Cornwall he had heard many stories about Cornish nationalism and how fiercely protective they were of their heritage, so when he first arrived he struggled to fit in and settle into the rhythm due to these stories. Despite sharing half of his blood with the natives of his new hometown, he couldn't shake that feeling of being a foreigner. The Cornish locals often joked about the high influx of foreigners moving into the village and Leif later learned this term meant the English. Like many villages in Cornwall, Mevagissey was a place where the much beloved St Piran's flag was displayed with pride and Cornish nationalism was not an uncommon thing. Leif was made very aware of this when his mum would tell him tales of Cornwall's history when he was a child. It was because of friends like Bruce and Dexter and Glenda that he felt welcome from the beginning, and he soon learned that the reason why the Cornish were so protective of their heritage was because Cornwall and its history were worth protecting.

It did not take long for him to be a fully accepted member of the little fishing community.

'You scared the hair off my bollocks Bruce! I was in my own little world,' said Leif who was feeling relieved that he had been pulled out of that nightmarish world of blood and fish. 'No, I haven't dyed my beard, why?'

'It looks a lot darker than usual,' said Bruce. He stepped into the aquarium, a large gentleman with a freshly shaved baldhead and grey stubble on his face. His pale complexion and faint freckles indicated that he was once possessed of ginger hair in his youth.

'Not working today? I swear you're a part timer these days,' said Leif with a laugh.

'I have to give my assistant something to do! Besides, with this storm and constant snow there aren't any new boats coming in, though I hope it's finally stopped for good now,' said Bruce. He stooped to peer into one of the tanks and inside he saw cod gliding back and forth, with lobsters scuttling at the bottom. Bruce stared with curious scrutiny. 'I wonder if they look back at us with the same wonderment when they see such odd forms of life looking at them through a transparent barrier.'

'You always say that,' said Leif with a grin.

'That I do my boy. Why do we need to search the outer realms of space when we have aliens living on our very planet beneath the strange seas?'

'I ask myself that very same question when I'm out catching specimens on the Siren.' Leif paused. 'Are you just passing by today or is there something I can help you with?'

'I was just passing by. Went for a walk along the rann wartha this morning,' said Bruce, using the Cornish term for 'highest quarter' and referring to Hitler's Walk when doing so. 'It's hard to believe someone was murdered up there recently, someone close to the community. The snow has wiped away all trace of the horror that tainted that spot. My family roots date back to the foundation of this village and in all those years there's never been a brutal act of murder like what happened that day. The worst you'd get back in the old days was brawls between rival fishermen and the occasional sabotage of boats.'

'Well, I suppose the smugglers used to suffer their fair share of death,' said Leif moving on to the next tank.

'Oh yes but nothing like what happened to Glenda.' Bruce fell silent. Saying her name reminded them both of the reality of the tragedy.

'I'm afraid to go up there now Bruce,' said Leif turning to look at his friend. A worried expression marred his face. 'That place has already got its fair share of ghosts roaming the steep banks and now it has one more. Glenda is now but a ghost of a Christmas, there to remind us of the loss we suffer at this time of year.'

Then, like a blow to the brain with a pickaxe of ice, Leif's mind was alight with a moving image of thick stumpy hands using her lifeless body to make a snow angel in the pure snow, contorting Glenda's corpse into a piece of ghoulish art like something one would find at a post-modern art exhibition. He saw her dangling while her blood drained into the snow angel. He saw an image of himself as a monster, an atrocious elf, an abomination of Santa. Leif's beard began to itch again and he scratched until the flesh underneath was raw. The pain stopped the images chiselling through his brain and driving him to madness.

'I don't know why you can't just shave it off,' said Bruce who startled Leif again. 'It would drive me bloody mad with all the irritation those things cause.'

'I would say that is why I get all the women but I don't.' Leif laughed. His face could not hide the sadness he felt.

'I'm detecting there's some trouble in paradise?'

'Your detector should be beeping like mad. Phoebe left me the other night. She said she felt like we needed a break and that I shouldn't contact her until she feels that it's the right time. I feel trapped like a disabled octopus stuck in a jar and unable to slip out of the cracks to freedom because my tentacles are flaccidly impaired.'

'You should let her go. There's no way I'd let a woman, or anyone, treat me that way. She's obviously confused as to what she wants in her romantic life and she shouldn't keep you trapped in that jar.'

'Then why bother to keep me around at all? Why not just tell me it's over and be done with it?'

'Most of the time when a woman, or anyone for that matter, says they want a break in the relationship it means they're too afraid to properly end it. So, she'll keep you in this limbo until you end it for her. It's harsh but it's the truth.'

Leif looked away from Bruce and finished feeding the aquatic animals. The sound of filtering water in the tanks dominated the silence and echoed on the walls. Eventually Bruce took his leave and left Leif alone with his thoughts.

Six

When he arrived home Leif went straight for the advent calendar perched on the Cheshire Oak drinks cabinet in the living room. It was a whisky calendar containing various miniature bottles of single malt that Leif opened each day and poured into a tumbler glass with a single block of ice. The calendar itself was of a curious design. Leif had picked it up in a whisky specialist shop in St. Ives earlier in the year. It was a wooden box with little doors, each with a little brass number upon them. Stood at the top was a nutcracker doll that appeared to be wearing the robes and crown of a king, and it held a faux glass of whisky in its hand. Leif thought it was cute but something about its eyes made him feel slightly uncomfortable, almost like it was watching him. It was a preposterous thought he had to shrug off every time he looked at it. The middle window of the calendar was number 25 and a smidge taller and wider than the other doors meaning a special bottle lay within. It was an expensive purchase but as Leif had said to the store clerk: 'Christmas comes but once a year.'

He sat by the fireplace sipping the whisky in his plaid-grey dressing gown, contemplating his comings and goings during the Christmas period. His mother, two sisters and brother were due to fly into Newquay airport from Norway on the twenty-third day of December. His mother was a Mevagissey native by birth and had moved to Norway in her twenties to look for work. It was there she met Leif's father, who was a French-Norwegian farmer. She fell in love with him and the country and stayed. Leif had grown up hearing stories of the quaint village and made it his mission in life to visit his Cornish roots and the place where his beloved mum was born. There he had met Phoebe, a Mevagissey native, he fell in love with her and the village and stayed.

In his dreams the Fjord horse appeared again. It trampled over a field of flesh where the grass was streaks of skin and the flowers were eyeballs on sinewy stalks and bushes made of clawing hands. The horse grazed the grass, and as it champed the unnatural crop viscous blood clung to its teeth. The beast was starving, its ribs on display in some act of cruelty, the horse slowly freezing until death claimed it as a beast of burden for the afterlife. As the

32

horse lay down to settle into its death, a hideous nightlight of bloodied stars blinked in the night sky, darkening for a moment before reappearing red and horrific. Leif woke scratching his beard and felt like it would catch fire from all the friction. He sat up on the edge of his bed and wiped tears from his eyes.

'Poor Didushko, why now?'

Yet again he considered shaving his beard off. He ran to the bathroom and snatched the electric razor from the shelf next to the sink. As he held it in his hand the reflection of his face in the mirror became something unholy for a brief span of time.

In his eyes was the image of Christmas in the form of a devil.

He dropped the razor on the floor then splashed his face with cold water and when he looked again the devil had fled from the pupils of his eyes. The concept of shaving his beard fled from his mind. He withdrew back to bed where the nightmares lurked, only this time he was left alone, and sleep was more like a void of darkness between two realities.

The sun shined for the rest of that week. There was no heat, the snow did not melt, and treacherous ice formed on the pathless narrow roads of Mevagissey.

On the eighth day of December Leif Fabian woke to the soothing sounds of Christmas carols. Outside the lighthouse a brass band had set up against the glistening ocean and performed to a small audience of onlookers. Herbert Hunkin was looking after the aquarium that day. He volunteered now and again when he wasn't doing his boat tours, to help ease Leif's work load and allow him some time off.

Leif ventured to the lighthouse to bask in the autumn sun and soak in some Christmas cheer. Lord knows the village needed it. Though the set up was purely instrumental with no singers the gathering crowd helped to fill in the vocal gap and the harbour was filled with sweet singing.

'The stars in the bright sky looked down where he lay…'

Leif approached the classic melody of Away in a Manger and joined in the makeshift choir at that line. The frosty breeze in the air and the brass band's audibly aesthetic music sent pleasant festive shivers through his spine. The people all around him were snugly dressed in thick coats and woolly hats, with scarves wrapped tight around their necks, their faces wore smiles and their breath exuding in plumes of mist. Lovers huddled together and families embraced to shield them from the cold. In that moment he missed Phoebe and wished she could have been there with him to sing Christmas carols in the sunlight.

The stars of fate are looking down upon you Leif, said a voice. It sounded like it came from inside his head. He did not recognize the voice so he surmised that it must have come from someone standing nearby. He looked around and saw no-one looking at him. Everyone's eyes were fixed on the band. Leif stroked his beard and tugged it three times slowly, something he did whenever he felt agitated. He broke away from the group and started climbing the steep winding stairs just off the pathway that led up to Hitler's Walk, deciding it was time to put his fear to rest. The climb exhausted him every time he attempted it, but the views when he reached the top were worth it. Leif held onto the rod of arctic ice that was the railing, taking each step with care. The coldness seeped through the fabric of his gloves and he had to snatch his hand away when the temperature sank its icy teeth too deep. Each step was a pillow of snow with a layer of slick ice beneath. The whole weather situation in Mevagissey puzzled Leif; it was unnatural, with even the locals remarking in astonishment at it.

When he reached the rann wartha his breathing laboured into deep gulps of air and long exhales of mist. There was no one else on Hitler's Walk. There was only Leif and the silence of the dead. He looked out over the village and saw the mounds of snow atop the roofs of houses, his included, and in that frozen mass the houses sparkled like gems as the winter sun reflected in a dazzling display of delicacy. The music from the brass band was distant, but he could still hear the tune of carols drifting on the chilly wind. The snow crunched underneath his feet as he edged ever closer to the spot where Glenda was murdered. There was a feeling of familiarity, like a false memory had been implanted in his head as a dream that he once thought was real. There was a split across his thoughts. He was crippled with a plague of falsities and moving images of gore twisting her corpse into the fashion of a fountain. Leif turned from the scene of the crime and ran for the coastal path. It was a relatively hidden path tucked out of the way of Hitler's Walk and despite being called a coastal path it did not stretch across the coast, but ended with a viewing platform a few feet from the gate that reached out from a cliff edge above Mevagissey.

The platform at first looked like a bridge, straight and narrow, but instead formed into a circular viewing dock where one could stand and look out in awe at the ocean, and the far-stretching coast of Cornwall. Leif ran to the platform and walked with steady steps across to the viewing dock. The sea breeze swept his face and cooled the frightful fever in his brain. Down below he saw shreds of rock splayed out in the water, looking like dragon claws stomping their doom upon Mevagissey. The waves lapped serenely against these craggy bits and Leif wondered what it would be like to leap from the platform and plummet onto those protruding shards of cliff.

If you did that then the fun would be over too soon, said that voice again. Leif whirled around and saw nobody there.

'Who said that?' he called out. Only the gulls answered with their reprehensible squawks. He grunted a nervous laugh.

'You're being a fool, Fabian,' he said to himself and stepped off the platform and made his way back into the village.

He walked a different way, taking the road down Polkirt Hill. This was a deliberate move on his part. Because the road took him past Phoebe's house. It was a curious house situated halfway down the hill. Its pebbledash exterior had been painted crimson, its front door painted a deep cherry red with a cast iron doorknocker shaped like a goat's head sitting below a cast iron angel, whose arms were spread in a welcoming gesture, seemingly appeasing that sinister goat. Above the door set in stone was a human face twisted with a mocking smile. It was the kind of eccentric theatrics Phoebe was known for and the inside of her house was no different.

Leif carefully navigated his way down the steep hill and watched his footing. On a normal day the pathless road would be busy with cars and Leif would need to stop regularly to let them pass. On that day the roads were too dangerous to be driving on. Especially Polkirt Hill.

Outside Phoebe's house Leif stopped and stared at the door. He knew she wasn't in, he knew she would be working at the museum, but suddenly Leif felt drawn to that house. Not because he was pining after his estranged girlfriend, but because some otherworldly force beckoned him.

The stars of fate, he thought, recalling the words of the mysterious voice that had spoken to him earlier. He took a step towards the crimson building and instantly stepped back and out of his trance when a car came trundling up the hill towards him.

'You mad bastard,' he said under his breath to the oncoming car.

In the afternoon he relieved Herbert of his duties and assumed command of the aquarium for the remainder of the day.

As time ticked away around the clock, advancing the hours into days and the days into Christmas, someone in Mevagissey was unaware that they were living their final hours within this mortal coil. A terrible death awaited them.

As the sun plunged below the horizon and dusk tainted the land, dark clouds congregated in the heavens in a conspiracy of dread. Those who had been out in the streets of Mevagissey celebrating the end of another week decided to go home as the great omen in the sky declared yet another storm. Village locals had taken to calling it 'the supernatural storm', since no meteorologists could predict its coming and going amid the abnormal savagery which it inflicted on Mevagissey.

On the night of the eighth day of December there was a deafening howl of wind, like Fenris-wolf had come to call on Odin for their final battle to the death. A whirlwind of snow fell in a fury and Leif lay in bed listening to the cacophony outside while Pink Floyd flowed out of the Bluetooth speakers on the desk in his bedroom. He was unable to sleep in fear of suffering from more hideous nightmares.

'*Wish you were here,*' he sang to the ceiling, thinking of Phoebe and how she would nuzzle her head into his shoulder on stormy nights.

When he did eventually fall asleep it was unexpected and unpleasant, and he dreamed that he pulled back his curtains and peered outside into the night. The lighthouse was blinking on and off and Leif noticed an abnormality on it which was difficult to make out amidst the swirling snow. It looked like a big star with a few little stars shining through it. There was a tinge of red emitting from the light like a maroon filter had been placed on the lighthouse window. It was like an eerie nightlight that bathed the village in a discomforting glow. Outside in the storm he heard carollers singing Away in the Manger.

'*The stars in the bright sky looked down were he lay...*' they repeated the line over and over again. The carollers were dead, dressed in Victorian attire with faces gaunt and chunks of flesh slithering off their bones, while pilchards protruded from between their ribs gasping with their moist mouths. Behind them stood the Fjord horse, the one his father had named Didushko.

Leif could smell the decaying flesh of fish and human and horse, retching before waking in a cold sweat to find he had vomited in his sleep.

Seven

It was early morning when he woke from the unsettling slumber, and his head was pounding with a steady rhythmic knock that penetrated his innermost sensitivity. After he had cleaned the contents of his stomach from the bed and placed the sheets in the washing machine in a half-asleep daze, he was sickened to find that the pounding persisted. It penetrated the void and slammed its way into his waking world and manifested into steady knocks at the front door of his little house by the harbour. Leif wrapped himself in his dressing gown. The deathly chill of the morning had shocked his naked flesh when he threw back the sick-stained bed sheets. He lumbered towards the door feeling like he was hungover despite only having a single whisky from the advent calendar the night before. Leif yanked open the door and a grim gust of freezing breeze struck his face and made his eyes instantly water. His friend Dexter Kloppers was standing on the doorstep looking windswept, his long hair dishevelled and his face aghast.

'Leif somethi…Jesus man what the hell are you feeding that thing?' he exclaimed in shock.

'What are you talking about?' asked Leif. His state of mind was fuzzy.

'Your beard man, it's HUGE!'

Leif stroked the vast mass of hair growing from his face and felt that it had grown exponentially overnight.

'How odd,' he mumbled. 'Anyway, what's wrong?'

Dexter didn't reply straight away, the dark and luxurious forest of hair transfixing him. It was to him like the whole world had melted away into a puddle of obscurity. Leif said his name sternly and questioned again about what was wrong. Dexter snapped out of the trance and his eyes immediately welled with tears.

'I'm sorry man I don't know what came over me. It's Bruce. Something's happened to him…oh god Leif it's horrible,' he said as the horror crept on his face like insects of doom.

'What's happened?' asked Leif looking at his friend with grave concern. Had he peered over his friend's shoulder he would have seen the gathered crowd and police presence across the harbour.

'He's been murdered. His body is on the lighthouse. It's pandemonium…' before Dexter could finish Leif ran out of the house in nothing but his dressing gown and slippers and trudged through snow and slush to the lighthouse on the other side of the harbour. The sky was swollen with grey clouds.

 The police were finding it difficult to keep onlookers at bay. Yesterday morning people had gathered to watch a brass band perform Christmas carols and now they were gathered to look at a gruesome and sadistic scene of a murder so foul, it made certain people faint on the spot or vomit into the water. Some of the younger rubber-necking folk held up their phones and took pictures or filmed like vultures swarming a carcass. Leif felt disgusted and wanted to snatch their phones away and dash them on the floor. It seemed that no one had respect for the dead anymore. His knees turned to jelly when he beheld the horror on display and he fought against the tide of unconsciousness and won by the skin of his teeth.

 'Oh my god,' was all he could say when he saw the body of his friend Bruce Huxley. It was a pure manifestation of malice. His gory naked corpse was strapped to the lighthouse over one of the windowpanes and his arms and legs had been spread to make his body look like a star. Star shapes had been cut right through the flesh of his torso like someone had used a cookie dough cutter. The wounds were neat like whatever implement was used had sliced into his body like a hot knife through butter. But the horror did not stop there. The lighthouse used to be an ivory beacon painted a glorious white and was maintained thoroughly by volunteers. On the ninth day of December crimson stars had been painted onto the white column with Bruce's blood. It was a deformity not only to Bruce's body but also to the whole village of Mevagissey. At the foot of the lighthouse Leif spotted a bucket of blood with a horsehair brush next to it. The brush was covered in thick maroon plasma and Leif remembered his dream and the horse that had been haunting him. He followed the trajectory of the direction Bruce's body was facing and it was pointed in the direction of his house.

The stars in the bright sky looked down where you lay, said that ominous voice. Leif grabbed his beard and scratched it frantically and suddenly it felt like there were creatures crawling around inside it.

'Who would do such a thing?' asked Dexter who stood next to Leif.

'A monster,' said a woman in front of them. 'No human could do such a thing, especially in Mevagissey.'

Leif put his hand on Dexter's back and led him away from the crime scene.

'Are you all right Leif? I wish you hadn't come here. I was going to tell you to stay at home before you went dashing out the house.'

'I'm not all right Dexter and not just because of this. I've been having these dreams both when I'm asleep and when I'm awake. They're like these visions of death. I see myself killing Glenda on Hitler's Walk in one vision then someone else doing the deed in another. I don't know how to make sense of what I see in my mind. Last night I dreamt about seeing a star-like shape on the lighthouse tinged with red, like the North Star had been painted with the blood of sinners, and then I wake up and see Bruce like this! Not to mention that both of their bodies share the common theme of facing towards my house! What the hell is going on Dexter?'

Leif's friend looked with pity upon the man who had lost two of his friends.

'You're distraught, man. You're full of grief that you haven't properly exorcised, and your mind is weaving this fabric of guilt because you couldn't prevent their deaths, which you shouldn't feel guilty about. No one could have prevented this.'

'Then what about last night's dream? How do you explain that?'

Dexter could not answer because he did not know how to begin explaining it. Instead he looked out over the harbour and tears tumbled from his eyes.

Leif left out the part about the voice talking to him. It was a mystery that couldn't be explained by anyone.

I think I'm going mad, he thought.

Not yet, said the voice, but you will be before Christmas is out.

Think of the devil and it shall appear.

Eight

On the tenth day of December the morning was a formidable freezing temperature and in the church of St Peter the full congregation had to huddle up on the pews to stay warm. The vicar delivered her service and prayed for Bruce Huxley and again for Glenda Cartwright.

'Though their deaths may have been sudden, we must all take some comfort knowing that they will live on in the kingdom of heaven,' she said. 'For God has given us all eternal life beyond the veil of this one.'

Leif did not attend church that morning instead he spent that Sunday mourning in his own way, by drinking. When the Fountain Inn opened that afternoon, he sat with Herbert and Dexter and ordered a round of whisky so that they may raise a glass to their fallen friends. It used to be that conversations in a Mevagissey pub would focus around fishing, the state of tides, boat building and the effects of tourism on the village. They were simple conversations for a people wanting to live simple wholesome lives, but the days had grown dark in every way, with their talks turning to nothing but murder and conspiracy. Rumours began to spread about who the culprit might be. People had their suspicions that it was an outsider, someone who hated their way of life and was making a statement by killing native members of Mevagissey. The rumours ranged from logical conclusions to outrageous ramblings that made people scoff in disgust. Leif couldn't help but think that Daphne du Maurier would be proud, the living turning into characters akin to her own creations.

'But no human could be capable of such evil,' said Herbert during one of these conversations. 'How could evil possess a mortal soul? This is the work of something beyond our understanding, an angry spirit spurred on by revenge. For what cause, I don't know, maybe we have upset it somehow by allowing our home to become a tourist destination, instead of staying as a traditional fishing and boat building village like the good old days. It's no secret that tourism has replaced what we were always meant to be and in the not-too-distant future our true purpose will be nothing but a board of text in the museum, where kids can only use their imaginations instead of actually seeing for themselves the marvels we once achieved here. What I know for definite is that this isn't over.'

For the most part his remarks were ignored and some guy on another table joked that Herbert had drunk one too many pints of Tribute ale. Folk in the village were familiar with Herbert's pagan beliefs. He referred to himself as a full-blooded Mevagisseyian, since the village had strong pagan connections dating back to its foundation. Leif listened to this conversation with a keen attentiveness and during Herbert's statement he resisted the urge to scratch his beard that was burning like a witch at the stake. He thought of his dreams and of his visions and became afraid to sleep again because he knew at some point he would see his own hands murdering Bruce Huxley.

Paranoia grew like fungi in the dark and damp corners of the community consciousness and folk began to regard one another with wary eyes. They tried to carry on as normal but evil was spreading in the village like plastic in the ocean.

Mevagissey was forever changed.

Nine

The build up to Christmas is often better than the actual day itself. This is an opinion voiced mainly by the older generations because to them time moves too fast and before they can blink another Christmas has passed and another year falls from the calendar as apples fall from a tree.

It was during the build up to Christmas one year ago when Leif met Phoebe Marley. It happened on the eleventh day of December when Leif was perusing his favourite bookshop, Hurley Books, on Jetty Street. Back then he didn't have a beard and his hair had been thicker and fuller so he did not have to wear a woolly hat to cover his shame. Hurley Books was known for stocking a plethora of interesting and unique literature, ranging from the popular to the classical and to the rare to the factual. That particular day Leif was leafing through a hardback book on marine biology. He had a passionate interest in all things that dwelled beneath the ominous ocean waves and since buying the aquarium he wanted to brush up on his knowledge. The owner of Hurley Books was a beautiful Greek lady called Lina who always caught the affections of the older gentlemen who frequented the shop. To Leif she was a literature companion and they would speak at length about local writers, especially Daphne Du Maurier, who was Lina's favourite author and the reason why she had moved to Mevagissey. She had visited Chapel Point several times in the years she had lived there and told Leif on numerous occasions to go, but so far, he had not. On that fateful day of the eleventh Lina was not in shop. Instead, it was an employee Leif didn't know, so he focused his efforts on browsing marine biology. Christmas music played quietly through the shop speakers and tinsel glistened on the bookshelves. In the window there were books pertaining to the festive season. In the central section of the bookstore there stood a cute Christmas tree that was decorated with wooden carvings of Nutcrackers, Santa, Reindeer and Snowmen, with a hand-made angel stood proud upon the tree's pinnacle.

Leif was engrossed in the text he held in his hands and was unaware that his destiny had walked through the door and was approaching him.

'Excuse me could I get past please?' spoke a voice that was like the ambrosia of sound to his ears. Leif looked up from his book and was stunned by her beauty, her long auburn hair and chestnut eyes shimmering with moisture. At first, he did not move, but became suddenly aware that he was gawping. The auburn lady smiled at him with warmth.

'I'm sorry,' said Leif and stepped aside.

'It's quite all right,' she said and stepped past him through the narrow gangway.

He smelt her perfume. It was soft and fruity and he fell in love with that smell instantly. For a while they stood next to one another in silence both enraptured by the books they were perusing and then the auburn lady broke the silence.

'What are you reading?' she asked.

Leif looked up again and was once more captivated by her chestnut eyes. This time he smiled and did not gawp.

'Oh, I'm reading about fish…and stuff,' he said and cringed at the words he chose to speak. The auburn lady smiled again and giggled.

'Fish and stuff?' she said with a grin.

'Marine biology, sorry, I'm buying a few books so I can reacquaint myself with a passion that's been lying dormant for a while. What about you?" he asked and nodded to the open book she held between her hands. It was a large hardback book that looked like it had some weight to it.

'It's going to sound weird, but it's a book on occult magick and rituals? Not that I'm into any of that stuff in a practical sense, but I'm interested in the theory behind it and the spiritual aspects of such practices,' she said and blushed as though she were embarrassed of admitting such a thing. Leif held her in high esteem.

'Sounds very interesting, though I don't know much about it I admit. Maybe we should grab a coffee and you can tell me all about it?'

The question just slipped out and before he had a moment to realize what he was asking it was too late. The auburn lady laughed. It was not a cruel laugh but one of surprise and flattery.

'You don't even know my name sir,' she said and put her hand in front of her mouth in an attempt to look horrified. Leif thought she looked cute.

'Phoebe Marley, at your service,' she said and extended her hand, which Leif took gladly.

'Leif Fabian at yours,' he replied and they both giggled.

'So I suppose we should exchange numbers and arrange this coffee huh?"
she asked and produced her phone from her bag.

'Well I was thinking now if you're not busy. I'm certainly not.'

'My, my, you work fast,' said Phoebe and flashed a cheeky smile.

'I was always taught to strike while the iron is hot.'

'The iron is most definitely hot sir,' she said with a smile of seduction that
filled Leif with warmth.

They both departed from Hurley Books without buying anything, heading to
The Wheelhouse, having coffee and a couple of slices of Stollen by the
harbour as they spoke at great length about each other's lives and interests.
Leif received a crash course in the occult and Phoebe got a crash course in
marine biology. She told him about her work at the museum and how she
dreamed of opening up her own museum related to Cornwall's history with
the occult. Leif listened to her intently. He was fascinated by Cornwall and
in many ways preferred it to Norway though the latter would always be his
real home.

'I just love to stand on the edge of beyond,' said Phoebe, 'to perceive life through a different lens and believe there are forces at work beyond mankind's shackles of science and organized religion.'

'Cornwall is definitely a place that stands on that edge so I think you're in the right place,' said Leif.

Phoebe nodded and smiled.

'Why such an interest in underwater wildlife?' she asked after taking a sip of her coffee. A thin line of foam stuck to her top lip like a milky moustache and she wiped it away with delicacy.

'I own the aquarium across the road,' he said pointing to the blue building with his thumb. 'So I've been wanting to get back into educating myself on the subject.'

Phoebe raised her eyebrow in curiosity.

'Oh really? You know how to impress a lady,' she asked and giggled.

'Nothing like a tank full of smelly fish to get a woman going,' said Leif and they both laughed.

'I'm sure I read that in Cosmopolitan. On a serious note I think it's great that you work with animals. I myself am a staunch advocate of animal rights.

I believe mankind's treatment of nature and its wild inhabitants can be despicable and we need to do more about it, so I think it's sexy that you have a love for them too,' said Phoebe and tipped him a wink.

What was originally meant to be a coffee ended up being a meal and night out and at the end of the night Leif walked Phoebe home and was surprised to find out where she lived. He did not go inside, not until their third date.

TEN

A year later on the eleventh day of December two days after Bruce's murder Leif found himself at work thinking about that fateful day and how he and Phoebe should be celebrating their one year anniversary.

'It'll be lonely this Christmas,' he sang to himself and something inside him made him feel like a pathetic mess.

No one ventured near the lighthouse for a long time. It was an unholy talisman, a stain on the village. The image of the bloody stars painted on the white column and the body of the severely maimed harbour master had warped the people's minds like acid had been thrown onto their brains. All were afraid to go near it.

The snow was deep. Leif's feet were almost engulfed as he walked home from a boring day at the aquarium. The sun was sinking but there was no dazzling effect in the sky; instead, the day dimmed into a grey twilight and the monochrome clouds above made everything seem darker. Leif thought of Phoebe and like a spirit being summoned by his call he saw her walking along East Wharf from the museum. He stopped in his tracks and stared at her. She did not see him and her attention was completely on her phone. A part of him wanted to run up to her and say hello, but he knew it would be a bad idea due to her explicit demand of them not having contact with one another. So he disappeared up the South West Coastal Path and to his house. The coastal path was elevated above the East Wharf path and from up there he saw Phoebe pass by like a phantom in the twilight, had she looked up she would have saw him peering down at her like a phantom himself. Her attention never drifted from her phone and his heart was broke in twain. It was their one-year anniversary and they weren't together.

He wondered if she was thinking about him and he shook his head in doubt.

Like all supernatural storms that have never happened throughout history, the one in Mevagissey became exceptional. In the sky lurid cracks of lighting shattered the heavens like the gods themselves were smashing the clay of their creations. Thunder growled with inhumanity and there was no rain, no wind, there was only more snow and Leif was baffled by the outrageous climate of the approaching winter. His dreams once again quaked with the heavy clomping of horse hooves and a grey beast of monstrous majesty sought revenge across the Norwegian fjords of his subconscious. It climbed mountains of metal and passed through impenetrable barriers of thought and in its fur crawled millions of lice that drove it to murderous madness, which only propelled it faster towards its purpose.

Leif unconsciously threw pillows at the walls and grappled with the duvet while muttering incoherence in his sleep. His beard throbbed with each pulse of forked light in the sky. Sweat beaded on his flesh like undesirable pimples waiting to erupt.

An almighty clap of thunder ruptured the dreadful dream and Leif bolted awake. His beard felt like it was crawling with the same lice that had been in his dream and he decided enough was enough.

It was time to trim that bulging bush.

The temperature in the room was deathly especially at three o'clock in the morning. Leif stood in front of the bathroom mirror and stared in wonder at how long and thick his beard had grown. He felt guilty for wanting to trim it down but the irritation was becoming too ghastly to bear. The electric razor vibrated in his hand and deeper vibrations quivered in the heavens outside. As he brought it up to his face a flash of lightning filled the bathroom and

Leif jumped. It felt like there was some kind of opposing force trying to prevent him from trimming his beard. His hand shook with uncertainty so he took a deep breath thrust the razor onto his beard and as it clipped a couple of strands of hair an unearthly cry of surprise erupted from those follicles. It startled Leif into letting go of the razor and it crashed into the sink and from his beard fluids of red and green squirted into the bowl and turned into a vibrant gold when they mixed in the sink.

'What the hell was that?' he asked his reflection.

I said ouch, a voice spoke.

It came from inside his beard!

Leif looked in the mirror with a mixture of astoundment and nauseating horror as a pair of tiny chubby hands parted his beard like it was a stage curtain. Leif's body shook like discarded leaves in an autumn breeze. He retched at the appalling sight and a squeamish chill nearly crippled his legs into collapsing and he held onto the sink for support. The next thing he saw appear from his beard was a pair of eldritch eyes with green sclera, blood red irises and white pupils that were so stark they could have pierced holes in the very fabric of his being.

Leif was paralysed in disbelief.

You made me bleed. Why did you go and do that? The creature said and Leif smelled the sickly aromas of candy canes on its breath though he couldn't see its mouth yet.

I'm still dreaming, thought Leif. *I've had a false awakening and this is still my dream.*

One of the chubby hands whacked his nose and Leif cried out in pain. The little bastard had a lot of strength it seemed.

You're not dreaming sonny, it said, this is about as real as it gets.

Leif grabbed the razor and went to sheer off his beard, but the thing spoke again.

I wouldn't do that Leify ole pal, you see if you cut me off then you die, we're bound together you and I until the bitter end. Your bitter end.

'What are you?' asked Leif.

What I am is of no importance right now. I wasn't going to reveal myself until the end, it was meant to be a Christmas surprise, but you had to go and spoil it. For now, you can just call me Tommy.

Then using its tiny hands, it pushed its face out of Leif's beard and to him it looked somewhat like a gnome. Its nose was flat with a scarlet sheen, its lips like pink slugs, and when it smiled it revealed a mouth crowded with square teeth that were stained yellow. Leif reeled in horror and when he went to grab it with his hands the imp withdrew with uncanny speed back into the beard.

You won't catch me that easy for I have deemed your destiny, Leif Fabian, and you can't ensnare destiny with your hands.

'What do you want with me?' Leif screamed at his reflection.

All in good time you scoundrel. I have to keep some things a surprise for Christmas Day.

'It's you, you're the one who murdered Glenda and Bruce!'

Stop spoiling the surprise! Yes, it was I and there will be more bodies come the Day of Yule. Now, be a good boy and go back to sleep.

Leif stumbled in a half daze back into the bedroom and collapsed into a dreamless slumber.

Eleven

The morning of the twelfth day of December Leif awoke from his deep slumber and remembered the events of the night before. He ran to the bathroom and looked into the mirror and saw that his beard was shorter. It was still bushy and brown, not blonde like it should have been.

I thought I'd do some landscaping for you, said Tommy. Since you were so adamant last night to trim it. It'll grow back soon enough. Bit of a waste of time really.

Leif sat on the toilet and placed his head in his hands.

'So it wasn't a dream,' he said and felt exhausted from the unusual debacle that had entered his life.

No, it wasn't a dream, buddy, so you best get used to having me around, until you eventually die of course. The clock is ticking, it said and then laughed in guttural grunts.

Leif sighed and got himself ready for work. He was too tired to be pondering his dwindling mortality and wanted to regain some normality in his life after the bizarre revelation from last night.

When he stepped outside, he saw that the snow had been replenished and was for the most part undisturbed. The pure white brilliance disturbed him a little as he thought about the terror coursing through the village that December and that his beard was the source of all those evil things.

This is a beautiful village, said Tommy. It's a shame your actions have changed this quaint place forever.

'What do you mean my actions?' Leif said aloud. He realised he had said that out loud and looked around to make sure no one heard him. The streets were quiet.

Don't worry I can read your thoughts Leify, I am a part of you after all – and as for your actions, you'll soon come to understand, although you're a bit of an idiot for not understanding already.

Why not just tell me for God's sake!

For *God's* sake I will not say anything, especially considering my god is Santa Claus and I hate that flabby mass of oaf. I'd spit if I didn't love your beard so much.

So you're an elf then if Santa is your god?

Ha! If I were an elf, I would mince my giblets and stuff them in my anus! Moronic little vermin they are. You know I'm glad we can converse like this, Leif ole pal. I was worried you would go insane and throw yourself off that viewing platform up there. I wouldn't blame you for doing so, but it would ruin everything.

I'm still holding onto the hope that this is a dream.

You'll be sorely disappointed. Oh, look, here's the aquarium, how exciting. Leif furrowed his brow in suspicion at this comment and opened the aquarium door. When he turned on the lights he released a blood-curdling scream.

There was nothing else he could do.

Looks like you'll be closing early today, said Tommy and it peered out of Leif's beard with a fiendish grin that was smothered with delight.

TWELVE

'In all my years on the force I've never seen anything like it,' said Police Constable Dave Shipley as he slugged back a shot of whisky in the Fountain Inn.

'Didn't you see the last two murders?' Dexter Kloppers asked. The two men were sat at a table opposite one another. The candlelit room made the atmosphere more ominous and it was like odious forces refused to allow a great amount of light to enter the room.

'No, today was my first day back on the force. I'd been on such a lovely holiday in Italy with the family and then I had to come back to this carnage. If I had known I wouldn't have come back.'

'What was it like?'

'Oh it was lovely absolutely beautiful weather. The kind of place you could retire to if you had the money.'

'No not the holiday! The crime scene.'

"Oh. Well, I'd rather talk about my holiday. Listen, I'll tell you, but this is the last and only time I tell someone about it, and it's only because you and I go way back Dexter. The scene was like something from a horror movie. When I first entered the aquarium, I saw that the first tank on the right as I walked through the door was full of blood. There were no fish or any sea life in the tank they had been replaced with slices of orange and sticks of vanilla and cranberries and wedges of lime and…and on top of the tank was a ladle…a goddamn ladle! Like the sick son of a bitch was making Christmas punch!'

Dexter's face was twisted in fright and the image in his mind made him feel sick.

'Jesus,' was all he managed to say.

'Jesus wouldn't allow something like this to happen,' said Dave.

'What about the body?' Dexter asked, but he didn't really want to know the answer.

'The body was in the opposite tank, naked, bloated and bruised looking like a discarded waxwork model and the fish were nibbling at him like it was damn buffet time for them! If I didn't inherit such a strong constitution from my mother then I would have hurled all over the floor. A couple of the

officers there had to step outside to do so. It's Christmas for heaven's sake!
The rest of my life is going to have to be spent in therapy.'

Dave Shipley ordered another round of drinks and the two men raised their glasses.

'To Herbert Hunkin,' said Dexter and drank deep.

'To Herbert,' said Dave. 'The poor old bastard didn't deserve to go like this.'

The pub went deathly silent as someone walked through the door. Dexter turned around and saw Leif Fabian enter the room, and darkness seemed to gather around his being.

'Dexter, I need to talk to you,' said Leif approaching the two men sat at the table in the far corner of the room.

'Sit down Leif. I'm here for you buddy,' said Dexter and he moved along to the next chair to make it easier for his friend to grab a seat.

Leif's face was disfigured by an eternal worry and he looked on Dave Shipley apologetically.

'I need to talk to you alone Dexter,' he said.

Dave took this comment as his cue. He stood up and sat down at a different table with some people he knew. He was off duty and though the police officer inside him was curious as to what Leif had to say, he gave the men some privacy so he could drink his troubles away.

'What do you want to talk about?' asked Dexter.

'We're friends right?' Leif asked. The question came unexpected to his friend.

'Of course we are. Why?' said Dexter.

'Because I am going to tell you something and it's going to sound fucking weird and you'll probably laugh but it's the truth,' said Leif.

'What is it?'

You're making a foolish mistake, Leify boy, said Tommy.

'Did you hear that voice?' Leif asked and his eyes were full of longing that his friend had heard the voice of evil.

'I only hear your voice,' said Dexter who was now looking more concerned for his friend.

They can't hear me Leify ole chum, only you can. You should probably stop now before Dexter-boy here carts you off to the loony bin and they lobotomise you.

'My beard!' Leif said raising his voice above Tommy's.

Dexter flinched.

'What about your beard?' he asked.

'My beard is a frigging serial killer!' Leif said through gritted teeth.

There, he said it. It was done and out in the open. Leif breathed a little easier for doing so. Now he had to suffer the fallout.

Silence descended on the two friends.

The reaction was to be expected, Dexter laughed, he didn't mean to, but it just came out. He suspected Leif was going to have a break down due to the recent events in Mevagissey but he didn't know the extent of that break down. Now it seemed Herbert's death was the mince pie that gave Santa the heart attack. His laughter was an involuntary reaction to an absurd statement. Leif wasn't angry with this because he knew his friend would not

71

understand. He had to tell someone though otherwise he really would throw himself off the viewing platform.

Your best friend thinks you're madder than Rudolph flying over Russia without air clearance, said Tommy.

Shut up, thought Leif and the imp did.

'I'm sorry man,' said Dexter who had ceased laughing once he saw the serious look on Leif's face. 'I don't mean to laugh but it caught me a little off guard.'

'Don't worry about it. I didn't expect you to believe me. I just needed to get it off my chest. It's true whether you believe or not,' said Leif and grabbed Dexter's pint and took a swig.

'Do you want one? You look like you need a drink.'

'No, thank you, I just needed to wet my whistle. I'm going now. I need to fully process what's been happening around here and find a way to stop it. How the hell do I stop a possessed beard? Christ. Maybe I should have shaved this damn thing when Phoebe told me to now it's a burden bringing grim death to this village.'

Leif stood up and before Dexter had a chance to call him back, he left the pub and ran home.

The faux log fire in the living room emanated a cosy heat and the amber electronic glow surrounding the logs was comforting. It was just a shame that Leif's state of mind didn't reflect that same comfort. He sat down on the sofa and uncorked a bottle of twenty-year-old scotch he had been saving for Christmas Day and poured a large glass and drank deep.

What a waste of a good whisky, said Tommy. You're a glugging fool Leify.

'Why Herbert? Why any of them? Why the hell are you doing this to me?' Leif cried out at the fire.

Don't be such a blubbering imbecile, man up and take your punishment. You wouldn't want to die with tears in your eyes.

'What do you mean punishment?'

Drink your whisky my old chum. I'm going to sleep for a while, as all good beards do from time to time. Don't you fret I will return soon enough. Sweet dreams.

Leif drank half of the bottle and woke the next morning regretting the decision to waste such a fine spirit. In his dream he saw the crimson house on Polkirt Hill, Phoebe's house, and on the walls were paintings of the Fjord

horse, each painting depicting it dead and in various states of its own

decomposition. In a dark corner of the room he saw the outline of Phoebe

and when she stepped into a jarring lilac light he saw that she was naked and

from her pubis grew a vast mass of hair that slopped onto the floor like the

tentacles of a dead squid. From amid the flourishing mass of pubic hair that

was entwining in and around itself into freaky wreaths, a pair of hands

emerged and cradled in them the skull of a horse. With inky empty sockets

dead like its flesh, dead like its bones, and dead like the strands of hair that

fell to the floor like suicidal fairies, it gazed upon Leif. Phoebe looked dead

too, her eyes bland balls of gelatinous goo that stared with false life, like a lie

told through the mouth of a freshly embalmed corpse. Her shoulders

quivered, her belly convulsed, and things seemed to be moving beneath her

faux flesh that one could have deduced were snakes or worms or a

conglomeration of things that slithered with sickening purpose. The hairs

slithered too, finding their way towards Leif. He could not move and the

hairs encased him like a cocoon preparing him for a ghastly transformation.

His eyes glazed over in panic, the pubic hairs were slick with a rotten smelling residue and his mouth opened to vomit but nothing came out and all the air was stolen from his lungs.

He felt suffocated and he woke just before he stopped breathing.

Thirteen

On their third date Phoebe took Leif to the Lost Gardens of Heligan, a spectacular botanical gardens one and a half miles outside Mevagissey. It was also the place where his best friend Dexter worked as a park ranger. It was a place Leif had heard a lot about but never actually got round to visiting. He was glad he waited because sharing the experience with Phoebe made it special. It was there they shared their first kiss beneath a tree where a mass of mistletoe grew. They both smiled and Phoebe looked up.

'It looks like a beard,' she said and giggled. Leif loved her smile and her perfect teeth and the way her chestnut eyes twinkled with mirth. He too looked up at the mistletoe.

'Don't you find it strange how it has become synonymous with romance during Yuletide, but mistletoe is really just a parasite that dangles from its host and saps away its nutrients?' he said. Phoebe giggled again.

'You're right and it's what killed the Norse God Balder, since his only weakness was mistletoe. It's synonymous with fertility and death, humanity's two inevitabilities,' said Phoebe wistfully. 'Maybe that's why we cherish it so much during the best time of the year. On a subconscious level we see life's cycle encased within those white pearls of fruit and are reminded that every beginning has an end and every death is followed by the birth of something new.'

Leif smiled at the auburn-haired woman standing in front of him. Her skin was as pale as the snow upon which they stood and in her eyes he lost himself to love and it became his inevitability. They kissed again underneath the mistletoe.

That night Leif was allowed inside her house and he marvelled at the décor when he stepped through the cherry red door.

'I walk past this house quite a lot on my little hikes up to Hitler's Walk and every time I would be fascinated by its unique appearance, and then I would wonder who lived in such a house. Now not only do I know who lives in a house like this I am dating that very owner,' he said and chuckled to himself. 'Do you live here alone?'

Phoebe hung up her coat by the door and took Leif's too.

'Yes I do. My parents left it to me. They died three years ago during the winter when they were out at sea in my dad's sailing boat. A storm caught them off guard and they were lost to the tide,' she said and ignited the fire.

A real log fire. The interior of the house had a very vintage look to it and Leif guessed that much of the furniture was antique. There were glass cabinets filled with interesting artefacts that were either historical trinkets or items pertaining to the occult. Leif then realised that he was standing in the early stages of the museum that Phoebe wanted to open.

After Phoebe had given him a guided tour of the house they sat in front of the fire and drank red wine with a fine selection of cheeses and biscuits to nibble on. They talked for a good while then eventually Phoebe led him into her extravagantly decorated bedroom.

'Now you can take a peek through my keyhole,' she said then immediately burst into fits of laughter. Leif laughed too at the absurd remark.

After the laughter they made love.

Fourteen

The next week in Mevagissey passed by like God had set His VCR to fast forward. Over the weekend a Christmas market had arrived in the village and the narrow streets were flooded with locals and tourists alike all indulging in festive foods and seasonal bric-a-brac. It was the only weekend when cars weren't allowed in Mevagissey. Leif had not heard a peep out of the creature living in his beard and slowly he began to wonder if it had all been a product of his distressed mind. But, his beard had grown again, at length, and it was a reminder that it was all too real.

On the sixteenth day of December, a Saturday, he left the house to explore the market, to free his head of the burden of sadness and allow himself to enjoy the final countdown to Christmas.

Amidst the hustle and bustle there was a group of teenage boys tucking into juicy bratwurst sausages, and the smell stirred the hunger in Leif's belly. He decided to buy one.

'That'll be £6 please, sir,' said the young lady at the counter. Leif took the expensive hot dog out of her hand and passed her some money.

'I'll have to mortgage my house now,' said Leif and laughed awkwardly.

The girl smiled sarcastically and handed him his change.

One of the teenage lads stood next to him.

'Whoa dude! Your beard is a monster!' he said.

Leif looked at him and raised his eyebrows.

'You have no idea,' he said and walked off with his bratwurst.

The dense crowds of folk going hither and thither through the market poured a potent potion of claustrophobia into Leif. He darted down Jetty Street, which was clear and sought refuge in Hurley Books. Lina was working that day and Leif said hello to her and they briefly exchanged the usual pleasantries that acquaintances were wont to do. There was nothing in particular he was looking for, so after a short period of deliberation he decided to make his way to the fantasy section and peruse the Tolkien books. He walked past a shelf that was loaded with Christmas literature both for adults and children alike. His eye caught something, a children's book with a vibrant cartoon cover and the title with the accompanying image set his teeth on edge and glaciated his blood in a river of ice. It was called The Naughty Nisse and the illustration on the cover was of a gnome-like creature whose face looked all too familiar to Leif. He scolded himself for not having made the connection straight away when seeing the tiny creature's face.

I know what you are you little bastard, he thought and grabbed a copy of the book and took it to the till. His beard gave no reply.

'You're a bit old for children's stories,' said Lina with a kindly smile.

'I know, but this is a little bit of home. A Nisse is a creature from Norwegian folklore. They look like garden gnomes, yet they're slightly different, not as cartoonish and they're mischievous little buggers. My dad used to tell us stories on Christmas Eve about the Nisse and warn us about being naughty, otherwise the Nisse would come and bite us, poison us, and once you're bitten there's no cure save Santa's forgiving grace,' said Leif.

'That's a brutal story to tell you kids', said Lina.

Leif laughed and nodded in agreement.

'Yes, it is, but it worked and sometimes Dad would put a garden gnome in our rooms just to frighten us when we woke up on Christmas Day. It was his way of having a laugh.'

This time Lina burst into tears of laughter when the image of little Leif screaming in terror at a garden gnome popped into her head.

'He sounds like a real character,' she said.

'Yeah, he was. They were simpler times back then, you'd wake up and open your presents and not have to worry about all of the stress that comes with Christmas, because you're a child, and the adults took care of everything. Then you blink, and suddenly you're the adult and it was like your childhood was just a dream that you've recently woken from – and though Christmas is still the most wonderful time of the year, you realise that it's also the most stressful,' said Leif.

'Don't start having an existential crisis in my shop, I won't tolerate it,' said Lina and she looked at Leif with affection. 'Besides, I don't know why you're complaining, you don't even have a family yet, wait until you have kids, then you'll know stress at Christmas. That's what my mum used to say.'

'That's even if I live long enough to have kids,' he said under his breath.

'Excuse me?'

'Oh nothing. Sorry, Lina. The crowds today have frazzled my brain. I'll get my existential backside out of your hair,' said Leif and he handed Lina some money. She pushed his hand away.

'No charge. Consider it your present, and besides I like having you in my hair, existential or otherwise,' she said and once again smiled with affection. 'I'm loving the beard by the way. I love the grisly look on a man. I reckon you should decorate it with some of those beard baubles. I've seen them online. I could order you some,' she winked.

'Thanks Lina but I think that might irritate it,' said Leif and smiled as a person would, who's told an inside joke.

'Well, it's a thought. I think you would look cute. Get some glitter on it too and it would be like you're wearing a Christmas tree, only upside down,' Lina giggled at the thought.

'I guess that makes me the angel at the top then,' now it was Leif's turn to wink.

Lina blushed.

Leif knew she had feelings for him, and he liked her too… the only problem was that he couldn't bring himself to let go of Phoebe, not while there was still a chance of them reconciling.

Their eyes lingered on one another for a while until another customer stepped through the door and disturbed their moment by stamping their snow-laden boots on the welcome mat.

'Thank you, Lina. Merry Christmas,' said Leif.

'Merry Christmas to you too, Leif,' said Lina and waved goodbye.

At home he read through The Naughty Nisse. The story was about a Nisse that became angry at Santa when his elves had stolen vegetables from its farm and were not punished, so as revenge the Nisse bit as many children as it could on Christmas Eve, poisoning them and Santa had to race around the world to heal them while delivering presents as well. Santa understood the Nisse's anger and punished his elves accordingly, but also dished out punishment to the Nisse who had reacted rashly by replacing its cabbages and potatoes and carrots with lumps of coal on Christmas Day. Lessons were learned and eventually everyone lived happily ever after. It was nonsensical and unusually dark for a children's story.

During his read through of the book Leif expected his beard to make some kind of remark about the surprise being once again spoiled.

There was only silence and a dull itch.

Fifteen

Tommy didn't make an appearance until the nineteenth day of December. The temperature had plummeted and now perilous black ice formed on the streets. Folk trod with caution and the elderly mainly stayed home, not wanting to risk severe injury. There were mounds of snow at the sides of the streets like deadly dunes of cold and some of these mounds were stained brown from dirt. Though the aquarium was closed Leif still had to go there to feed the sea life and check on the tanks. Opening the door was like trying to move a tremendous boulder. The heaviness of Herbert's death weighed on his mind and crushed his ability to face the inside of that blue building. When he turned on the lights a flash of the incident ruptured his thoughts, with a deluge of blood and nibbled flesh entering the gates of his cognizance. Leif braced himself at the doorway and then entered. Though everything had been cleaned thoroughly no fish or crustaceans had been reintroduced to the two tanks at the front. To him they were tainted with doom.

He fed the fish and left as quick as he could.

At home he stood in front of the full-length mirror that stood in the corner of his room. His face was somewhat sunken and he had lost considerable weight in a short space of time and Leif realised that he had hardly eaten since the murders started.

You should get some food in your belly old buddy especially since your time is coming to an end. You'll want that coveted last supper. His beard spoke at last and Tommy appeared through the curtain of hair. It pushed itself out further this time and Leif saw that its beard grew into his. The two of them were entwined in the follicles of fate.

'You've decided to grace me with your appearance then,' said Leif and he sighed in disappointment.

The time is nigh and I bet it drove you mad. I bet you were questioning whether I was actually real or not. Well unluckily for you I am real.
Leif rolled his eyes.

'How do you even fit in there?' he asked.

People of a more primitive disposition would call it magic, but a more scientific mind would call it an inter-dimensional vortex. Kind of like Mary Poppins' bag but with more hair, said Tommy.

Leif burst into laughter and immediately hated himself for finding that psychotic critter humorous.

'I know what you are now,' said Leif after calming himself down.

Oh, do tell, said Tommy, and stroked their beard with curiosity.

'You're the Naughty Nisse.'

This time Tommy burst into laughter and sound was shrill and full of mucus.

Nisse, yes, I forgot that's what you Norwegians call me, though I prefer the Swedish version, Tomte, hence why I call myself Tommy. My kind has been called many things over the vast span of years. As for naughty, I find that rather slanderous, I am just doing my duty after all.

'And what duty is that?'

Tommy smiled and revealed those yellow square teeth and tapped its nose thrice with one of its chubby fingers.

I want you to slowly digest all of this, so your stomach knots with the anticipation of the sheer dread that awaits you.

'Please don't murder anyone else,' said Leif. The plea slipped out, now that the absurdity of the whole situation was gone, and what was left was the raw understanding that there might be another body before his was put on display.

'Whatever grudge you have against me take it out on me, not anyone else, please.'

The eldritch eyes of the Tomte were full of indifference and cruelty.

I'm sorry, Leify, but it is part and parcel of the punishment. You have to reap the harvest of your wrongdoings. There will be more bodies come Christmastime.

'What the hell have I done that's wrong? Tell me so I can atone!' Leif screamed.

Tommy the Tomte chuckled and smelled their beard then disappeared back into the forest on Leif's face.

Frustration thumped through him and Leif clenched his fists until there was pain. His hands were red and the indentations of his fingernails remained as crescent craters for a brief time. Meanwhile over Mevagissey the sun was bowing out of another day and bidding farewell until their next meeting. Another snowstorm assaulted the village and Leif fell into another sleep full of distressing dreams. This time he was on the old family farm and inhabited his childhood body. He was standing by the Fjord horse named Didushko by his father, and he brushed its majestic mane. He had to stretch his arm to properly reach. Disushko was his best friend, they shared an exquisite bond of beast and boy, and Leif could not wait for the day he could ride him around the fields, imagining he was a great warrior from some fantasy tale. But Didushko was dead, no breath came from his mouth, and his body was cold and frozen in a standing position. Over the quick course of minutes his body became as ice, and the hairs of his mane fell apart like brittle bones under the brush. Leif felt compelled to keep stroking Didushko and he found himself brushing way the horse's frozen flesh. Slowly the cold skin was sloughed off until there were only icy muscle fibres and raw ridges of rouge that could have been canyons for microscopic organisms. The brush was worn down to the wooden handle and Leif stood back and marvelled at his creation. It was a piece of organic art that would remain a taboo forever in his heart.

He woke up crying.

Sixteen

While Leif Fabian was sleeping through a morose nightmare, Dexter Kloppers was finishing off his last round at The Ship Inn, a nautical themed pub located on the corner of Market Square. He had drunk more than he intended to that night, and the conversation in the pub had once again turned to murder and mutilation and the head-scratching pondering of who could have committed the violent deeds. The weather outside was becoming frightful and when the snowstorm suddenly descended he decided it was time to retire to his home. He was still wearing his park ranger uniform, having gone straight to the pub after work at the Lost Gardens, intending to only have dinner there, rather than the skinful of booze that instead found its way into his system.

The usually dark and narrow roads of the village were illuminated with the colours of Christmas from the fairy lights dangling outside of houses and shops. Dexter tried to walk with steady feet but in his inebriated state he swayed to and fro like the boats in the harbour. A couple of times he skidded along the pavement, once by accident and the other deliberately after finding the first time fun. He talked himself out of a third time, so much had happened in the village recently that he didn't want to tempt fate upon himself.

Dexter lived along River Street, the main stretch of road that eventually led out of Mevagissey, in a house that was opposite the main public car park. He still lived with his parents at forty years old. It wasn't wholly by choice though. After a failed marriage that was triggered by the loss of his only child five years ago, Dexter returned to the family home to recover his mind and ended up staying.

The thick falling snow obfuscated his vision, and the occasional gust of wind that blew in his direction made it more difficult to see what was in front of him. The streets were silent and it was almost apocalyptic, as if he was the last human alive on a planet of ice. Something caught his eye through the falling flakes, the shape of which he could not make it out at the distance he was at. It looked like a tiny person of sorts. When he got closer he saw it was a statue of a gnome perched on a stone pillar outside someone's house. It was something he would have noticed many times on his way home.

'Must be a new addition,' he said as he scrutinised it. The gnome was painted gold and in its hand it held a tiny St Piran's flag. Dexter thought it looked cute.

'Even the gnome is a nationalist,' he said and chuckled. Dexter never saw himself as a Cornish nationalist, he had travelled the world too much in his youth to build a wall around his open mind. That's the way he saw it. He came from the old hippy school of thought and tried to love everyone he met and engage in reasonable debates, which was becoming increasingly difficult in the modern era of social media. So he decided not to be a part of that technological generation. He chuckled once more at the little golden gnome and continued his swagger home.

Behind him something smashed and when he turned around he saw that the gnome had been blown off the pillar and was now clay shards on the road.

'Poor little blighter,' he said in a mock Australian accent and giggled. The fairy lights strung up between the trees and wrapped around their branches flickered, and were suddenly extinguished. Dexter looked up, his face crinkled in drunken bemusement. The road was dark, the cold penetrated his beer coat, seeping under his skin, wrapping around his bones. Those shivers only added to the feeling that he was being watched. The tumbling snow made it difficult for his eyes to properly adjust to the darkness. He sensed something was close by, an interloper shrouded in black mist. Something moved against the snow.

'Yeah forget this, I'm out of here,' Dexter whispered to himself and he turned to walk away. Then the outline of something familiar appeared and Dexter's eyes bulged with disbelief.

'It can't be,' he said as the outline of a gnome walked through the snow flurry seemingly untouched by the flakes. It was like the snow was too afraid to touch it. At first the gnome was small, dwarf size, but the closer it got to him the larger it appeared to grow. Its beard was long, shaggy and brown, with streaks of grey under its chin. It wore crude boots of brown leather, a jumper made of some coarse burgundy fabric, and on its head it wore a sand-coloured hood with a pointy tip that appeared to be made of suede. Its eyes radiated a paradoxical glow of Christmas and malice, and when it smiled Dexter felt his body temperature fall to deathly levels. He turned and ran but instantly slipped and fell to the icy road. Blood spurted from his nose and a cold sharp pain burned his face. He stood up, the adrenaline and survival instinct spurred him on. When he tried to run again he found that his feet were frozen to the road, and he saw an icy mist emitting from the gnome's mouth. When Dexter blinked he thought he saw just for a fraction of a moment the face of his best friend Leif.

Oh my god it was true!

It was his last thought.

The gnome was upon him, its size had increased to behemoth proportions, standing eight feet tall and made of pure intimidation. Its beard launched at him, striking like a hairy squid and wrapping around his body, working its way into every orifice he possessed and penetrating him with an unholy ugliness. His eyes were wide with terror and as the tears fell they froze into tiny icicles. Dexter gazed into the giant gnome's eyes that were made of the colours of Christmas and its smile was full of sadistic joy. It thrust its flat hand towards Dexter and a searing loathsome pain opened a schism of blood and organs in his abdomen.

The Tomte began its work.

Seventeen

If his eyes had legs they would have severed their organic ties and propelled themselves out of his skull in an attempt to escape the horror they had seen. His words had scarpered and instead a dreadful silence came over him and all of the onlookers who bore witness to the latest body in Mevagissey. Police Constable Dave Shipley and his partner P.C. Catherine Baker were the first on the scene, both of them standing close to one another wanting to hold each other and sob at the frightening scene laid out like a botanical portrait before them. They remained stoic because their job demanded it and the weeping rubberneckers standing close by needed strong role models during this difficult time.

If this wasn't so messed up it could almost be considered a work of art, thought P.C. Shipley.

Outside the Ship Inn on the corner of Market Square was a large plant pot with the words **Property of the Lost Gardens of Heligan** stamped onto the side in a deep maroon. The clay pot was full of frozen blood and planted inside that gory block was Dexter's ruined corpse. His eyes had been gouged

95

out and inside the soulless sockets poinsettias had been planted in bunches. On his head was a crown of holly and fat berries that looked like they were bulging with blood grew from between the sharp pointed leaves. Dexter's torso had been sliced in two and opened like a book of suffering and betwixt his organs were bunches of pink roses and red poppies and mistletoe hung from the craggy tips of his snapped ribs. From his gaping mouth hung his tongue and it had been painted with garish yellow mustard and his teeth had been removed and replaced with small sticks of vanilla. His arms were lifted up and Christmas bells had been hung on his crooked fingers. It was later discovered that his stomach had been stuffed with cranberries and his bowels stuffed with sage and onion and his scrotum had been cut open and his testicles replaced with a pair of Brussel sprouts. It was so horrific and ludicrous that the coroner couldn't help but laugh. It was either laugh or go mad.

Constables Shipley & Baker did their best to maintain crowd control until the detectives arrived, but the streets were confined and claustrophobia inducing, and the vast concourse that was gathered seemed to be hemmed in by the buildings like the streets were closing in on the madding crowd.

'Move back please folks! And please have some respect and put away your phones,' shouted P.C. Baker.

The din was deafening and the mania of the village folk became almost unbearable to handle.

All was silenced when a heart-wrenching scream erupted from Fore Street.

The dreams were becoming ridiculous and more intense. Visions of a death he did not want to commit scorched the earth of his dream world with despair. In this dream he saw his hand slice into Dexter's abdomen like a keenly sharpened knife slicing through a wedge of cheese. His beard was once again alive like the serpents of Medusa's hair restraining Dexter's arms and violating his inner body. Blood drained in a strangely slow and controlled flow into a terracotta plant pot and icy breath froze Dexter's dying body and his face contorted with terror because he had seen Leif's face perpetrating the heinous murder. While he arranged the cadaver into a botanical and gastronomical spectacle the outline of the Fjord horse Didushko lurked in the shadows. He whinnied and stamped his hooves with bloodthirsty anticipation. The clip-clopping of those hooves upon the cobbled streets, the creaking of the saddle leather, and the dull sound of the Didushko cropping the flesh from a bed of Leif's beard hair echoed through the narrow streets of his dream and filled his mind with madness.

The icy breath that stemmed from his soulless mouth froze the blood in the pot and finally sealed Dexter's body in a gruesome destiny.

Before Leif woke up he saw the Ship Inn and he jolted awake in a state of panic.

'What have you done?' he whispered to the dim light of his empty room.

Only what you deserve, answered Tommy the Tomte.

Leif got out of bed and threw on his winter clothing, and after strapping his snow boots to his feet he ran to the Ship Inn. He paced down Fore Street and saw the top of Dexter's body over the crowd of people. The scream erupted from his mouth like the hand of Carrie and the sound soared over the heads of the local rubberneckers and startled them all into silence. Leif began to push his way through the congregation and as he burst through the human barrier P.C. Shipley stopped him from going further.

'I'm sorry Leif but I can't allow you,' he said with an apologetic look.

Like the crowd Leif too was startled into silence when he saw his best friend's body on display like some weird Christmas garden. His eyes were fixed on the detestable detail the poppies wove into the heart and the pink roses sprouting from the lungs and the…

Leif suddenly understood what was happening.

You're targeting the people I know and love you bastard, he thought.

The Tomte did not reply.

Leif looked away from the crime and scene and straight into Dave Shipley's eyes.

'I have to stop his,' said Leif.

Before P.C. Shipley could answer Leif turned and fled through the crowd in the direction of the harbour.

He fled towards the museum.

Eighteen

Closed.

The sign stopped him in his tracks. He knew she would still be in the building cataloguing and rearranging displays and updating the literature ready for when the museum reopens. Leif felt the nerves creeping underneath the flesh of his arms and legs, they quivered and his breathing laboured under the pressure of seeing Phoebe again. There was no time for second thoughts and no time for hesitation or anticipating the negative outcome of turning up unannounced at her place of work.

Death was coming around the corner with Christmas as its slave.

He took off a glove and knocked on the door, the wood clacking against his cold knuckles, the sharp bite of pain making him wince.

'We're closed,' a faint irritated voice resonated through the door. Leif's heart skipped a beat at the sound. He knocked again.

'The sign says we're closed!' said Phoebe and her voice sounded closer like she was on the other side of the door.

'Phoebe it's me, we need to talk,' said Leif. There was a moment of silence and he feared that she had walked off and left him out in the cold.

Then the door opened.

Phoebe's frustrated face peered out of the door and she looked on Leif with unkind eyes.

'What the hell do you want? I told you not to contact me,' she said. Her breath was as cold as her words.

'Dexter is dead,' he said. Phoebe's face wavered and her eyes welled with a flicker of sorrow.

'I'm sorry to hear that. Is that all?'

Leif was startled by her icy inclination to his upsetting situation.

'Look, I know you said you didn't want to see or hear from me but I thought this would be a good enough reason. I know you liked Dexter and I think you might be in danger. All the murder victims have been people close to me. Something has got it in for me Phoebe and I'm worried that your life isn't safe here. Yes some*thing* not someone. I can't explain it but there are supernatural forces at work here. A terrible darkness has crept over the village, and it has targeted me for some nefarious reason I can't seem to fathom. You have to get out of Mevagissey, not for long, just long enough so I can try and stop this,' he said and his eyes pleaded to her warmer side. They pleaded for her to listen.

Phoebe did not budge.

'I said I'm sorry to hear that, Leif. I would have found out the news regardless of you coming here. Word travels fast in this place. As for me being in danger you're being ridiculous. You always used to listen too much to Dexter's conspiracy ramblings and now you think you're in an episode of the X-Files. I thought better of you. Why not just apologise for what you did and admit you were in the wrong, instead of making up some bullshit story to make me think you're some kind of victim and wannabe hero?'

'What I told you happened years ago! I apologised to those whom it affected. I can't change it. I paid the price.'

'No, you haven't paid for it, otherwise you wouldn't be living such a comfortable life. It's still fresh in my mind and for now I can't forgive you. You know my feelings and now I feel like I don't know you.'

The words stunned Leif into silence and he felt like a mannequin that had been forced to watch his fibreglass friends be pulled apart and rearranged in offensive positions, and could do nothing to prevent it. He could not exactly

say his life was comfortable, not anymore. Despite her stone-hearted

comments he still saw something in Phoebe's face that suggested she was

sad at the news of Dexter's death and in the end he nodded and walked

away. From behind him he heard the wooden door clack shut and the

disappointment in him rattled like a disgruntled snake.

He wandered aimlessly around the harbour fighting the urge to break down

and scream. He came to the lighthouse and it was still cordoned off and

looking like a monument of tragedy. He stared up at it thinking of Bruce,

and how his life had been so unnecessarily extinguished by a creature that

should not even exist.

There used to be a time when my people roamed the lands of Scandinavia,

said Tommy the Tomte. Leif felt his beard twitch and rustle. My people

lived side by side with humans for many a year. All we wanted was to farm

the land and live wholesome lives in peace, but our farms were often

plundered and our livestock slaughtered. The humans underestimated our

strength and our power, and we punished those who dared to deceive us and take advantage of our good nature. Eventually we fled into obscurity as the domination of humanity grew and their populations increased. I admire your newfound bravery in thinking you can stop me but it is only a delusion brought on by madness.

'I am going mad,' said Leif, still staring up at the lighthouse windows. The weather darkened and the waves began to crash against the harbour walls. The clouds swelled with snow and suddenly Leif knew what he had to do.

The supernatural storm returned and the superstitions of the village folk were solidified like the frozen blood in the terracotta plant pot. The snow tumbled to the earth like autumn leaves and soon fell in sheets that made it hard for the eyes to see.

'Will it never end?' said P.C. Baker to Shipley, as they managed to regain control of the crowd after the sudden storm. The people fled for shelter, some taking refuge in a café or pub and some darting for their homes where they planned on never leaving the fireside. The mangled body of Dexter Kloppers was slowly becoming something akin to a zombie snowman, which added to the absurdity of the whole thing. Dave didn't know whether to laugh hysterically or cry in the same manner. He threw up the hood of his florescent yellow jacket and pulled it tight around his face.

'I don't see the detectives getting to us any time soon in this weather. What shall we do?' asked Baker. She too had pulled her hood close to her face and it bunched her cheeks together and made her look chubbier than she actually was. Dave thought she looked cute.

'I'm not sure what we should do now. I should have stayed on holiday,' said Dave and he started to cough.

'And miss the chance to see Mevagissey's first ever serial killer get caught? No Thanks!' said Catherine and her face was beaming with an excited grin. Dave's face was only brooding with concern.

'I don't think this one will ever be caught,' he said. P.C. Shipley turned to look down Fore Street and his eyes glimpsed through the snow the shape of a red boat trundling through the harbour. 'Is that the Siren?' he asked in disbelief.

Nineteen

It was like being inside a snow globe that was being shook by an ill-tempered child. The waves crashed against the Saffron Siren like the moistened hands of Poseidon wreaking revenge on Odysseus. Leif's vision was severely hindered by the wall of cold white falling from the iron clouds above. He felt the stirrings of an enchantment begin to weigh his eyelids down so he slapped his face with an almighty force that shook tears from his eyes. It seemed to break the enchantment. Leif realised that it was the same spell the Tomte must have used to keep him in a deep sleep during the nights of its murderous carnage.

'No! Not this time you naughty Nisse!' he shouted at the storm. His eyes were squinted and he could just make out the daunting shapes of his destination and the destiny he had once envisioned.

It was worth a try Leif old buddy, said Tommy the Tomte. You've shown some remarkable resilience to my enchantment. I tip my pointy hat to you. So what's your plan then? To flee Mevagissey so no one else you love will be murdered? I'm sorry (not sorry) to say that it doesn't matter what you do, Christmas Day is fast approaching and you have an important date.

'At least no one else will die needlessly!'

My friend no one ever dies needlessly. There is always some twisted logic woven into the fabric of life. The deaths of your friends served a purpose a punishment for what you did.

'At least I can keep Phoebe safe!'

Ha! Dexter was the last so no need to get your beard in a twist. Speaking of beard…

A queer tingle fluctuated through Leif's face unlike anything he had ever felt in his life. He felt the Tomte rustling through the follicles of his beard like an explorer navigating through a dense forest. Then in his immediate vision he saw the little critter birthing from his beard. Its own beard was attached to his, and the two beings were for a time connected by an umbilical cord of hair. The Tomte severed that connection when it perched itself on the dashboard next to the boat's wheel. Leif thought it was a curious looking creature, looking like a garden gnome, and yet it looked nothing like a garden gnome at the same time, and its appearance was dishevelled like it had been working too many hours on the farm. It regarded its human host with those unsettling Christmas eyes and when it smiled Leif saw its teeth were stained with red.

'You monster! You fat little monkey!'

Hey! No need for name-calling!

'You fucking ate Dexter!' Leif retched and almost projectile vomited over Tommy the Tomte.

What are you talking about Leif old pal? I think you may have finally cracked like that silly bastard Humpty Dumpty.

'I can see the red stains of blood on your teeth!'

A fit of laughter was detonated from its little corpselike mouth like it was a fleshy bomb of humour. Tears of golden discharge spewed from the corners of its eyes and it thumped its tiny fat fists on the wheel.

What do you take me for some kind of wretched flesh-eating freak? I'm a vegetarian you nincompoop! The red stains on my teeth are from shovelling cranberries in my mouth while I was stuffing them into Dexter's stomach. I'm a sucker for cranberries. Their tang tickles me in ways you can't imagine.

Leif breathed a sigh that was a mixture of horror and relief. He stayed focused on his destination determined not to let the Tomte distract him, which he felt was the thing's intention.

I'm not trying to distract you, said Tommy reading Leif's thoughts. It doesn't bother me what you do it won't make a blind bit of difference.

Leif slowed the Siren slightly and pulled out his phone then dialled his mom. It rang for a few seconds and she answered.

'Hello mom…yes I'm fine…yes, yes…look, mom, I've got some bad news you're going to have to cancel your trip here…yes everything's fine we're having some really bad weather in Mevagissey and I think the roads are going to be closed with all the snow we're having…I know it's sad…no, no don't attempt it…no it's fine I'll just spend the day with Phoebe…well if it clears up I'll fly over to you for New Year…I love you too mom, tell the others I love them too and hopefully I'll see you soon. Goodbye.'

He felt terrible for lying to his mum, but it had to be done. It was the only way to keep his family safe. Mostly he just wanted to say goodbye.

They would have been safe. From me anyway, they wouldn't have been safe from the horror of identifying your corpse at the morgue though, said Tommy the Tomte.

Leif was close to where he wanted to be so he lashed out and grabbed the naughty Nisse in his hand and squeezed, intending to squish it like the vermin it was.

Tommy the Tomte yelped in surprise.

What in Santa's beard are you doing? It cried out.

The snow cleared just enough for it to see Chapel Point ahead of them.

'I'm going to crash us into the rocks and kill us both you little bastard!' yelled Leif as he squeezed harder. The little Nisse's face glowed red in both anger and suffocation.

The Saffron Siren edged ever closer to its fretful fate and the waves clashed with the craggy rocks beneath the famous house. A fierce battle of nature. The wind tried to thrust the boat off course and the ocean hammered from all directions, but Leif's expertise meant they stayed firmly on course.

'What is this, the fucking Truman Show? I know you're the one summoning this storm and you won't stop me! If I die then you die, like the pathetic parasite you are!' He began to laugh hysterically, before his laughter was overpowered by the Tomte's cunning chuckles. Leif looked at the tiny Tomte and saw in its eyes a daring knowledge, a dreadful awakening.

You truly are a simpleton Leify ole chap if you think I can be stopped so easily. If you were someone else I would have bitten you and you would wither and die. However I like you too much to inflict that kind of fate upon you, and it is a nasty awful fate to suffer being bitten by a Tomte.

Tommy the Tomte, that naughty little Nisse started to expand in size, and Leif had to let go of it. The once small critter was now becoming a full-sized monster growing in stature until it was two feet taller than Leif, who was already a tall gentleman. He looked up at it with fright and the Tomte looked down on him and smiled. When it spoke its voice was so deep and booming that it resonated through the boat's framework, and here and there bits of wood cracked and flung splinters every which way.

I'm afraid this is where it ends for you old boy, said Tommy the Tomte. Leif was stricken by asphyxiation then inky darkness.

He may have been resilient to the Tomte's enchantment, but he could not withstand the throttling nature of its beard.

TWENTY

'Why in God's name is there a bathtub in your dining room?' asked Leif as he walked through the front door of Phoebe's house. Beyond the door of the living room he saw a large cast iron tub at the centre of the dining room. It was another obscure addition to Phoebe's growing collection of curiosities.

'Technically it's a cauldron. I don't know why it's shaped like a bathtub,' she said and kissed Leif on his bearded mouth. She flinched away. 'Ugh when are you going to shave that horrid thing? You could hoard a menagerie in that wild forest. At least trim it down!'

'The day I shave this lush face fuzz is the day flying pigs replace the reindeer on Santa's sleigh,' said Leif and he chuckled. Phoebe was not impressed. He approached the room that harboured the strange specimen that was more bathtub than witch's pot, and as he got closer he began to see shapes carved into the obsidian iron. All around it like a metal tapestry were the depictions of little gnome-like creatures in the various stages of what appeared to be a day in their life on Christmas. It started with child gnomes peeking inside their Christmas stockings, and flowed into some gnomes playing the fiddle, some sat around a feast, and there was a long bearded gnome king sat on his throne holding a goblet. A fox lay at his feet, a group of gnomes marched with Christmas banners, and a family of gnomes gathered around a Christmas tree near a fireplace, with grandpa gnome was sat at a table smoking a pip, with the final depiction being of Daddy gnome tucking his children into bed. The tapestry started all over again in a continuous Christmas loop, a stream of Christmas consciousness etched forever into metal. Leif was baffled by the intricacy of the detail and the craftsmanship that must have been poured into carving the art into the iron.

'This is incredible,' he said, leaning in closer. He thought the gnomes were cute, before shivering as he realised that they were all in black. He sensed a sinister element at work. It was their faces. In one aspect he saw their smiles of joy and in another he saw contorted expressions of bloodthirsty murder. Like the meat at the feast was something other than animal. He started to feel dizzy so he looked away.

'It's early Victorian according to the lady I bought it off. Apparently, it was used merely as a decorative piece during Yuletide. She did add that it could have been used to make a potent Christmas punch for lavish parties,' said Phoebe.

'Is that all? Seems unlike you to buy something that's decorative and not affiliated with the occult.'

'Well since you mention it, the lady did say it was surrounded by a rumour that it may have been used to summon Christmas spirits to either reward the good or punish the bad. Personally I think those spirits probably came from the booze brewed in this thing. I can imagine this thing was only used at parties of pure decadence. I've never seen anything like it in my life and that is why I bought it. The museum would house more than just occultist items. I want it to house a miscellany of weird and wonderful paraphernalia.'

'I've never seen anything like it either,' said Leif and he noticed that the tub was supported by four ornate cast iron presents and the bows were wrought into the tub and flamboyantly flicked outwards at the corners to give one the impression that they could be unwrapped.

'I bet it was a bugger to get in here. I feel sorry for the guys who drew that straw,' said Leif.

'You have no idea. Want some mulled wine to bring in the Christmas period?' said Phoebe.

'You don't need to ask,' said Leif and he smiled tenderly at his lover.

It was the night before the storm and all was calm in Mevagissey, nothing stirred in the harbour not even a seal. The streets were dark, no Christmas lights were on, but all in the houses the village folk dwelled and kept themselves warm with fireplaces and television. In the pubs they drank beer and engaged in good cheer all waiting for December to open their advent calendars, to enjoy the festive season with rhyme and good reason, unknowing of the bloody terror that would soon change the village forever after.

It was the last day of November, and Leif and Phoebe were sat on the sofa. As the night waned, the wine in their glasses waxed and their tongues loosened and poured forth confessions.

'I think,' said Phoebe stifling a hiccup before she continued. 'Excuse me. I think we should tell each other the naughtiest thing we have done at

Christmas.' She giggled and the hiccup came out in full force. Leif laughed too and stroked her cheek softly.

'You go first,' he said.

Phoebe's face flushed red and she scrunched her face up in embarrassment.

'I must confess I was never much of a naughty girl, Mother and Father raised me properly so this may seem like the most boring thing ever. It was Christmas Eve and I was fifteen years old and all my friends at school had tried alcohol, they were going through that phase of experimentation and I was always left out because of how strict my parents were. Anyway on Christmas Eve my parents had been sipping sherry, and I asked if I could try some, to which they said no because I wasn't old enough. When they went to bed I sneaked downstairs and did a shot of sherry, it burned at first but the taste was delightful so I drank half of the bottle. My parents were woken by the sounds of me throwing up in the toilet and the bottle was on the bathroom floor spilling the rest of the sherry. My parents were angry but they laughed it off the next day when I felt like shit. They let me have Christmas but grounded me for New Year. I told you it was a boring story.'

Leif could not help but smile at her.

'You're such a little rebel,' he said and chuckled. Phoebe slapped his leg playfully.

'Okay then Mr Bad Boy, you tell me your naughty story.'

The sober Leif would have made something up, something that matched Phoebe's story but drunken Leif allowed his mouth to spill the words like the sherry in his lover's childhood bathroom.

He told her about the Fjord horse named Didushko.

TWENTY-ONE

Leif Fabian grew up on a farm in Bergen, Norway. It was the kind of farm tourists visited to take their children to pet and feed the animals, the kind of place that, during Christmas, set up a Santa's Grotto and brought in reindeer.

It was the year of Leif's twelfth birthday when his dad bought Didushko from a Polish gentleman whom he had named the pony after. Didushko was his father's pride and joy and Leif's best friend. By the time Leif had grown to full adulthood, the horse had too, and was a majestic hulk of a beast. His colour was grey dun, his mane was as black as night, and he ran with a speed that stole Leif's breath away whenever he rode on him. All the children loved to marvel at him and pet his mane.

It was the year of Leif's sixteenth birthday when it all went wrong.

It happened on a Christmas Eve and Leif, this tall and broad teenager capable of riding the fully-grown horse, had been traversing the land just outside of Bergen when a snowstorm ensnared the world around them. Luckily for Leif he was already an experienced rider and managed to

118

navigate both boy and beast back home safely. The adrenaline from the dangerous ride and the excitement of Christmas intoxicated his rational mind, and when he neared the family home on the farm he again saw the hypnotic decorations draped over the roof and windows. Through one of those windows he saw the Christmas tree and his family were inside presumably playing games, their faces were twinkling with delight. Leif longed to be inside, in the warming glow of the fireplace and in the warming embrace of his mother. Suddenly the thought of settling Didushko down in the stable seemed like too much of a burden, a chore he was not prepared to undertake. He dismounted a few feet from the house and patted his best friend softly and all around them the storm whipped and thrashed.

'You wait here my friend and I'll get Father to come out and settle you in the barn. Don't go anywhere,' he said to Didushko. There was nothing to tie the beast to and in his naïve youthful mind he expected the horse to behave and stay put. Leif ran to the house, occasionally turning back to make sure Didushko was there, but the snow was falling thick and fast and boy and beast were soon parted forever.

Leif's father was furious and he scolded the boy for being stupid. How could he just leave a horse unattended in a storm without an anchor to keep the animal in place? Father and Son ran out into the storm hoping against hope that Didushko was still where Leif had left him. It was no good. The horse had run away, probably scared by the howling wind. For four days the storm lasted and for four days they could not go out and search for Didushko. It was the worst Christmas for the whole Fabian family, all paid the price because young Leif was impatient and wanted to partake in some Christmas cheer, instead of attending to his responsibility first. It took them two weeks to find the half-buried frozen corpse of Didushko and by that time many animals had stripped away his flesh for sustenance in the cold climes. So scarred was Leif's father that never bought another horse, and Leif spent years trying to shake off the guilt of what he had done. For many years Leif kept Didushko's skull on display on his bedroom wall as a reminder for the wrong he did. Before he moved to Mevagissey he buried it in the section of field that Didushko loved to roam around when he was alive and full of strength. He held the skull in his hands, kissed it, tenderly, and said goodbye. After that he intended to move on and keep Didushko buried forever with his guilt but the ghost of that horse of Christmas past would always haunt him. It would haunt him to his grave.

When he finished telling his story tears shimmered in his eyes. His brain was throbbing with a heavy drunken buzz and there were still two hours left until midnight. Phoebe stared in stupefaction into those moistened orbs of truth and gradually the expression of utter contempt crept into every crevasse of flesh on her face.

'I think you should leave,' was all she could manage to say. She set the wine glass carefully down on the table next to the sofa then brushed her hands against her thighs in an attempt to retain a calm composure. Leif raised a puzzled eyebrow at her.

'Excuse me?' he asked.

'I think you and your disgusting beard should leave. You're a revolting human being leaving an innocent animal out in the snow to die. What were you thinking? Did you really think it was going to just remain where you told it? Are you a fucking idiot?' Phoebe's voice increased in volume with each question, which she spat at Leif like venom.

'I was young and foolish and I know that's a poor excuse but it is what it is, a moment of my life when I messed up and can't change it. For you to get angry now serves no purpose. I learned my lesson and I paid the price in my relationship with my father. He forgave me but never looked at me the same again.'

This confession did not move Phoebe. She only stood up, folded her arms and stared down at him. Her mind was made up.

'I don't think we should speak for a while. I need to think some things through, about us, about who you are. Consider it a separation of souls free to explore ourselves and our wants in order to discover whether we really are supposed to be together. It's something I have been thinking about for a while and I think tonight has clarified the questions of my heart. Maybe one day we will be drawn together again if my forgiveness can find you first,' she said.

Leif was astonished by the words pouring from her mouth and he could not find the words to defend himself.

'This is ridiculous! Things between us have been great and now…' Leif was about to throw himself into a maelstrom of angry words but stopped. It was useless to argue. Phoebe's eyes said everything he needed to know. He stood

up and gathered his belongings then walked to the door.

'Please don't try to contact me. When I'm ready I will contact you,' said

Phoebe as he opened the door.

Leif Fabian walked out of the crimson house on Polkirt Hill and would not

return until his fate was sealed.

TWENTY-TWO

The dream was a memory. The memory was a revelation. One he should have seen straight away. One he would have seen, if not for the love for the recently unobtainable clouded his rationality. As he roused he discovered that he was lying naked in a tub full of warm mulled wine.

A cast iron tub.

His mind was hazy and intoxicated, and his attempts to heave himself out were thwarted by that drunken sluggishness. The smells of Christmas spices slithered up his nostrils and in this liquid cocoon he felt a metamorphosis creeping upon him.

Don't worry Leify old buddy you deserve this, said the voice he had become unwillingly familiar with during the build up to Christmas.

A tiny fat hand stroked his sweaty brow and the Tomte regarded Leif with those menacing Christmas eyes.

I had to put you in a temporary coma. I'm afraid your little excursion to suicide forced my hand. It's the twenty-fourth day of December and I've got you on a slow cook.

Leif tried to speak. His words were slurred and incoherent. He was

malnourished and he found no solace. No strength in which to escape.

Tommy the Tomte smiled.

The cast iron cauldron was more bathtub than witch's pot, and was not

being heated by any conventional mortal manner. It was Tomte magick and

Tommy wanted to make its own Christmas brew.

Mulled wine with a special blend of Leif and spices.

Do you know what a Tomte's favourite animal is? Tommy the Tomte asked.

No don't try to answer you're not in a fit state my friend. Allow me to regale

you. The Tomte's favourite most prized animal in the entire wide world is

the horse. Is it becoming clear now?

Leif's eyes widened and he nodded like an out-of-it junky wanting another

slither of impure blood in his veins.

Tommy the Tomte continued.

I was summoned from the very cauldron you're boiling in because of the

heinous crime you committed against one Fjord horse named Didushko.

'I…I…' Leif tried to defend himself but the words would not form from his

gloopy brain. In the dining room doorway amidst all of the macabre paraphernalia contained within the crimson house on Polkirt Hill was

Phoebe Marley. She gazed upon her former lover with a look of treacherous

shame. Looking like someone who had plummeted too deep into an abyss

she did not mean to manifest so wide.

Leif furrowed his brow in anguish.

Phoebe crossed the threshold of the doorway and stepped carefully towards

the cast iron cauldron.

Her eyes flickered towards the Tomte and fear arose inside her.

'I'm sorry Leif. I never thought there would be so much death. You are the

one who deserved punishment, not your friends,' she said, kneeling beside

the cauldron before caressing Leif's cheek. Our poor protagonist breathed in

the alcoholic vapours and stared at the woman he used to love.

Steadily a new lease of life began to flow inside him, a sliver of strength

finding its way into his bones, allowing the curtains of inebriation parting

ever so slightly.

Tommy was squatting on the edge of the cauldron, smiling a devilish grin

full of those stained square teeth.

Isn't love precious? asked the tiny creature.

'There is no love between us,' said Leif through gasping breaths. The mulled wine was getting warmer and soon shifted into hotter temperatures. His flesh was painted crimson and sweat poured from his face. He breathed in quick jolts. He wanted to reach out and drag Phoebe into the cauldron with him but the strength in his limbs was not yet substantial enough.

'What I did was caused by an impulse of rage. As you cannot change what you did to poor Didushko I cannot change what I have done to you. Eventually you will pass out from the heat. There death will find you with no pain. Just fall asleep and save yourself the trouble,' said Phoebe.

She kissed his cheek and a flare of ruthless pain spread through her neck. Tommy the Tomte had bitten Phoebe Marley.

She looked at the creature with a face full of terror, dumbfounded, clutching at her neck. Leif suddenly felt life within his bones again and he shot up out of the tub. Meanwhile his former lover was convulsing, bent double, her hand clawing at her neck so hard she could have torn her flesh right off. For all Leif knew, that was what she was trying to do.

Blood bled into the backs of Phoebe's eyeballs, feeling an immense pressure building. She let go of the bite wound and grabbed her head, squeezing and

127

thrashing it from side to side. Her mouth was wide open but no sound came out. The pressure had stifled her vocal cords. The whites of her eyes flooded with crimson and blood leaked from her tear ducts and dripped down her face in streaks like war paint. Suddenly in the most repulsive sight Leif had ever seen her eyeballs burst like blood-filled balloons and even made a horrendous *pop*! when they exploded. Blood spurted every which way. That's when the screams were free to roam out of her mouth like herds of stampeding buffalo. She fell to the floor and this time thrashed her body about like a woman possessed. Blood spewed like projectile vomit from every orifice and flooded the floorboards with the hideous crimson plasma. Her skin began to pale and turned a ghostly grey and blue hue. The only vibrant colour on her body came from the bite mark. It radiated an eerie yellow glow that seemed to pulsate like insect larvae. From her mouth poured more blood. She coughed out in horrible guttural splutters and for a time her screams were subdued. In its place was a noise far more gruesome like the sound of a pot of thick bubble and squeak boiling away and making a rippling squelching sound as the temperature increases.

Leif wanted to be sick.

Now the floor was a pond of blood deep enough for a toddler to bathe in. It was obscene, it was nightmarish, and most of all it was upsetting to watch, as Phoebe Marley's lively thrashes became pathetic twitches. Her flesh became leathery and shrivelled like grapes in the sun and her veins protruded from that grey-blue skin like bits of brown string.

She flopped around in the blood pond like a gasping pilchard and then died.

Tommy the Tomte jumped from the cast iron cauldron and plodded on over to the distraught Leif who was holding his dead former lover in his arms and weeping openly.

I don't understand why you're so upset. She's the one who caused all of this, it said.

'Why did you kill her?' asked Leif through hitching sobs. 'And why haven't you killed me?'

I saw into your mind Leify old pal our beards were bonded on more than just a follicle level. I saw that you did not mean to send that horse to his death. You were an irresponsible imbecile not a malicious murderer. Poor old Phoebe here summoned me under the pretence that you had knowingly killed an innocent beast. She deceived me and I hate deceitful people therefore I had to bite her. I admit it was an impulsive act. Can't change it now though. You still deserved your punishment, for Tomtes love horses beyond all living creatures on this earth, and to see one die because of a human's ignorance to its nature should never go unpunished. But as a Christmas present I will grant you your life.

Leif nodded, 'Thank you, I guess,' he said.

Tommy the Tomte nodded back, its bizarre Christmas eyes twinkled with delight and it stroked its beard like it was dog.

There used to be ancient tales that us Tomtes were the original Children of Santa, long before the Elves, because we were created in his image, being of a very similar appearance. I think it is utter bollocks, Leif my pal. Santa cast my people out when the original Tomtes tried to free the reindeer. They said it was cruel to make flightless animals fly all across the globe in one night just to give presents to children whose parents were too lazy to go out and buy them themselves! Santa, being of a jolly disposition, chuckled at their remarks and slung my people out into the wilderness to fend for themselves and he laughed as he did so. Afterwards he created the far-too-happy Elves, these half-lobotomised creatures who are always happy to serve their master. Santa only wants to bring joy to the children of this world. He doesn't care who gets left behind during his once-a-year mission. I'm not saying he doesn't care about his reindeer because he does, in fact he bloody loves the buggers but that doesn't mean what he does is right. He's a fat blind old fool who doesn't understand why his reindeer keep dying and he has to keep replacing them. He's human just like you. All those ages my people thought he was a god but what kind of god would fling his children out into the open? Surely a god would care? And here I am punishing the bad while he rewards the good. I get the short straw even though I care about the animals, the real innocents, the ones who don't have a say in how they're treated. Where's the justice in that?

'You and Phoebe would have got along swimmingly had you not killed her,' said Leif.

Yes I know, but just as you can't change what you did to Didushko and she couldn't change what she did to you, so I can't change what I have done to her.

'I have to admit I'm a little taken aback by your existential speech just then.'

I always get a little melancholy after a Yuletide kill. Like when you open you presents on Christmas morning then instantly become sad that the best part is over. Goodbye Leify old friend. For now, said Tommy the Tomte.

Promptly it popped and became a million strands of beard hair that floated all around Leif. Slowly they descended like snow and fell with grace and twirled like helicopter seeds. Most of the hairs landed on the polished burgundy floorboards and thousands of fibres settled on the pond of blood and gathered into thick clumps of copper smelling slush.

Leif stroked Phoebe's hair and looked at her lifeless body in despair. He would never forgive her betrayal but he could not deny the love he once felt for her.

Slowly her body began to dissolve into a viscous gunky substance and the pond of blood transformed into soil. Leif stood up not believing what he was seeing. There was plant life sprouting from the clumps of blood-soaked hairs. Poinsettias and bunches of candy cane sorrels grew resplendently and their leaves opened and revealed the colours of Christmas.

A bittersweet smile grew on Leif's face.

'Goodbye Phoebe,' he said.

TWENTY-THREE

The supernatural storm did not return to Mevagissey and though it snowed on Christmas Day it fell with elegance and provided the village with a glorious white Christmas. Despite the grim events that had occurred in the village during that frozen December the locals still managed to celebrate. They celebrated the lives of those who had been lost forever, making the most of a Christmas that should not have been filled with so much death.

Leif didn't celebrate, though he did have a long FaceTime conversation with his family and was comforted by their voices. He told them the whole truth of why they couldn't go to Mevagissey. He told them about the murders and about Phoebe disappearing. No one knew that she was dead because no trace of her remains existed. Leif told everyone that she had ran away after the break up to finally build her dream museum. No one questioned him.

Leif left out the outrageous part about his beard being a Yuletide serial killer.

That was a secret he kept to himself forever.

A year later Christmas was much different. Leif had given his heart to someone special and he allowed himself to celebrate the Yuletide season. That special person was Lina, owner of Hurley Books, who had kept him company last Christmas during the aftermath at the crimson house on Polkirt Hill.

Leif held a special Christmas party at his little house the one that overlooked Mevagissey harbour. His family attended without anything supernatural disrupting their visit and they met Lina, whom they loved immediately. Leif kept his beard because Lina loved it and especially loved stroking it during their evenings cuddled up in bed. He never forgot his friends, those who had been murdered in such gruesome and unforgiving ways and he lit candles every Yuletide after in their memory. He tried hard to forget about Phoebe, the woman whom he had loved until she betrayed him using her extensive knowledge of the occult to try and bring about Leif's demise. Her treachery stuck to him like the flames on a brandy-soaked Christmas pudding, so for her he lit a black candle in order to banish her evil memory from his thoughts. It worked for a while.

He never forgot Tommy the Tomte, that disgruntled Christmas gnome, the thing that lived inside his beard during one cold and terrible December. Every Christmas he thought about that murderous and mischievous critter, that Naughty Nisse who caused him so much loss and insanity. He wondered if it was still lurking inside his beard, waiting for a moment when Leif would do something bad. Waiting to once again murder all whom he loved. Whenever he trimmed his beard he expected to hear a tiny yelp of pain, and see those menacing Christmas eyes peeping through the forest of follicles on his face and he would shiver with fright because he wished never to experience a repeat of that horrible Christmas.

The Christmas when horror had a hairy disposition.

The End.

BONUS CONTENT

THE NUTCRACKER KING DILDO

Prologue

Long ago in a time that existed somewhere in the dusty and forgotten corners of our simple human perception, there existed an illustrious kingdom full of luxurious creatures known only to the realms of imagination. This kingdom was ruled by a long lineage of smooth wooden beings known as the Nutcrackers, fully animated people full of soft organs and complex emotions, all tucked away beneath a hard varnished wooden shell. This is A tale of the Nutcracker King – or one of them at least, for none of them were ever given names at birth. A kingdom was their destiny, and their destiny was to rule.

However, I can tell you for certain that this particular tale is about the last of the Nutcracker Kings. He was the ruler who sent his kingdom to its first and final war with the mutated rats of Evange Galarr. Rats have a penchant for dismembering bits of wood, and Nutcrackers were particularly deft at cracking rodent skulls with their extendable, unyielding mouths. What ensued was a great and terrible conflict that left the once noble and cheerful kingdom drowning in a deluge of its own blood and sharp splinters. The

Nutcrackers were defeated and the Nutcracker King was exiled into the realm of humans, to be frozen in a state of permanent rigor mortis and left in some new-fangled hell where the world would pass him by and his only company would be his memories and regret. Nothing would set him free from the prison and nobody would ever love him, or allow him to love.

For many a long year he drifted, for some time he was used as a Christmas ornament in a nursing home, nobody could tell how disgusted he felt from the foul stenches of vinegar piss and excrement that had the aroma of rotting poultry and stale biscuits. The remainder of the year he spent in a cardboard box full of ancient decorations that never spoke and never yearned to be touched and held and comforted.

Those were his yearnings.

At some point he was finally handed over to a family where he was used as a garden ornament all year round, he would have found it a kind of haven if it weren't for the family dog and various nocturnal animals fouling over him to mark their territory. No amount of rain would ever make him feel clean.

One night he was plucked out of the ground by an arrogant fox that carried the Nutcracker King back to its den where it used him as a chew stick for some time. When the fox died he lingered under soft, moist dirt reminiscing the days when he saw the old folks celebrating Christmas and how some of the residents would ask the fake Santa Claus for a new wife who didn't have cancer, or a son who wouldn't abandon them in some strange building with strange people with no memory.

Eventually he was dug out of the ground by a gardener who was aged well into his 50s. The gardener was a gentle and caring soul who fixed the Nutcracker King up, repainted his body and gave him a new coat of varnish. It was the first time in forever since he had been given any kind of affection, but it didn't last long. The Nutcracker King was flogged at a car boot sale at the meagre price of £1.64 to some woman who owned an antique shop in a small town called Aurum's Desire.

He had drifted for a long, long time, but his luck was about to change. Soon, the Nutcracker King would meet Louis Thwaite, and everything would change.

1

Louis pushed the brass key into the lock of the door that opened his shop. He owned a small town sex shop called 'Follicly Endowed' on account of him having a magnificently shaped and bushy beard, and a big cock, not to mention his oversized ego that his girlfriend always said would get him into trouble. On this particular day Louis was not opening the shop for a regular day of business, he was only there to pull some money out of the till to fund his day out. Every year he hosted an annual Christmas S&M party for all kinds of sleazy and degenerate men and desperate post-menstrual women who just wanted some disgusting cock to make them feel whole again. Louis and his girlfriend never got involved in those kinds of parties, but the annual Christmas gig always raked in some extra cash for what would usually be the holiday blues. Louis needed some cash now out of the till so he could gather some equipment for the shindig, it was always good to have at least a couple of new toys to keep the punters interested, considering they were always the same punters, with the exception of a couple of curious students who would usually scarper out crying in either sheer terror or confusion. Before he began his search for unusual items that could be used in a sexual manner, Louis decided to visit his local antique shop, the aptly named 'Ancient Exposures.' He was always fond of antiques, he appreciated the history and culture behind something as beautiful as a grandfather clock or the way one could marvel over a simple object like a dinner plate painted by the proprietors of a distant time and country. He also loved the smell, that musty aroma that signified age and wisdom.

Louis rarely purchased anything from the antique shop, sadly being the manager and owner of a sex shop didn't make you a millionaire, especially in the age of the internet, which provided many sexual services for free or affordable prices. But he still enjoyed having a peruse, it reminded him of his father and of the days where life was simple and his family were around to catch him when he fell.

There weren't many new items in that day, the owner was a local woman named Betty Herod and she would often go to car boot sales and buy items she saw as valuable for extortionately low prices. Louis often wondered if she actually had a clue about the antiques trade, but in a small town he guessed it didn't matter.

Before he left the building his eyes caught a glimpse of an item tucked away between some creepy porcelain dolls. It was a nutcracker, he could tell from the shape of its mouth. It was like that of a ventriloquist doll and was shaped like a person and painted in the regal garments of a king.

2

"It's perfect."

The Nutcracker King heard the bearded man speak these two words that should have been three if weren't for the obnoxious abbreviation. He had been nestled between a pair of painfully angelic dolls that seemed to feed off the fearful energy children exuded when looking at them. It had been months since the kindly woman had taken him away from the car boot sale and positioned him on a special place in the antique shop, though customers who just wanted to browse had eventually moved him. He became increasingly frustrated at how these people could lead such blissful lives knowing they were shoving their collective middle fingers up at the woman for not purchasing any items. If only he could speak, if he only he could move, he would show them what would happen to insolent people if they were in his kingdom. The Nutcracker King felt the warm and slightly moist fingers of the bearded man touch his smooth wooden exterior, stroking and contemplating. He did not want to be bought; he didn't want to leave this comfortable home he had finally come to embrace. The fates obviously had other plans as the bearded man's large hand wrapped around his stiff body and lifted him out of the cozy soft spot between the dolls' legs.

Louis Thwaite could not believe his luck, for a long time he had been going to the antique shop, browsing through its odd and ancient items, yet he had never spotted this little beauty.

"It's perfect," he whispered and stroked the wooden toy considering his options. After a brief moment he decided he would purchase the item. A nutcracker was exactly the kind of thing he would want at a Christmas S&M party.

The owner of the antique shop quoted him the price of £45 stating that it was a rare item crafted using Birchwood long ago in Iceland. Louis was fascinated and slapped down his debit card eagerly; he could not wait to show his girlfriend and most of all he couldn't wait to see the punters use it at the party.

All this time the Nutcracker King felt his heart race and his stomach tumble with frustration, not only was this woman's origin tale a load of horse radish, the price she was charging was extortionate considering she had only paid the measly price of £1.64. Yet there was a part of him deep down that felt flattered that she considered him to be very valuable.

Louis departed and ventured back home satisfied with his one and only purchase. It would make a fine instalment to his collection, and he even made the decision to make it his official mascot during the other 364 days of the year. It would sit proudly next to his till and would be the King of Follicly Endowed.

3

"…in the frosty air…"

The Nutcracker King heard Louis bellowing the song. Christmas was around the corner, a period he had not had the luxury to fully appreciate without some disgusting aroma or unfortunate situation marring the occasion. There were talks of a party happening in Louis' strange shop and the Nutcracker King was brimming with excitement.

The day he was brought to his new home, the Nutcracker King was greeted by the smiling, yet somehow devilish face of Louis' female partner. Her name was Matilda Oswald and at first glance she dismissed the wooden toy as a waste of money, even when her bearded spouse explained the "origin" story she still did not seem impressed. Nevertheless she didn't kick up too much of a fuss, much to the Nutcracker King's surprise, that cheeky twinkle in her eyes gave him the impression that maybe she wasn't a force to be reckoned with. For a few days he resided in their single bedroom apartment, he observed that their relationship was, in the daytime, pretty normal, but in the evenings they often engaged in outlandish acts of sex. They rarely argued, though the Nutcracker King could tell that Matilda wished her companion had a job that brought in more income. Apparently he owned something called a sex shop and its name made the Nutcracker King laugh heartily within his mind. If only he could speak, if he only he could move, he would jump up and slap Louis on the back and chortle himself into a fit. At last he was introduced to his new and possibly final abode. The shop was full of bizarre items; phallic objects made from strange materials that looked like plastic but felt like flesh, unnaturally large rubber fists, clothes that not even a court jester would dress in, and moving pictures about girls having sordid affairs with their father's best friends, among many other ghastly genres.

Louis perched his mascot next to his till and sallied forth to begin the organisation of the XXXmas Annual Bash.

"…jingle bell time is a swell time…"

He sang heartily in the back room, it contained one king size bed, one triple sofa, yoga mats on the floor and a cabinet full of strange and exotic toys, mechanisms, and tasty lubricants. Louis called it the Treasure Trove and soon his brand new antique nutcracker would earn a place in there if it performed exceptionally on the night. After the mundane tasks of laying clean sheets and general domestic cleaning, he finally began to embark on the exciting task: decorating.

One of his particular favourites was a female mannequin doll he once rescued from a bin behind a retail store, he dressed it in tight red PVC, leaving the breasts exposed but he dabbed on a couple of sparkly nipple tassels. On its/her head he threw on a black Christmas hat that had the words "Bah Humbug" sewn into the white fabric, yes he even added a white beard! But the crème de la crème came in the form of an eleven inch black silicone strap on dildo that included wavy bumps on the tip. Sometimes the women liked to fuck it while sucking one of the guys, but in most cases it was the guys who liked to fuck it. Those kinds of fetish parties had a habit of pulling any straight guy out of the closet for a few hours.

 The Nutcracker King was given his first feature length view of the party room; it was a festive debacle designed to jolt the imagination into picturing the most heinous images. He was a gongoozler – an idle spectator at a spare no expense freak show, bound and gagged, unable to voice his distraught opinion to the production crew. The king sized bed had been fashioned into a tacky Santa's sleigh, attached to the foot of this prop were several black leather leads with spiked collars at the end, the Nutcracker King didn't even want to contemplate what they were used for. It was a strange affair, throughout all of the preparation he never really gave any thought to his role in this fabled Christmas party, he had always assumed he was just going to be another ornament forced to endure a wicked spectacle of decadence.

"...to rock the night away..."

At least his new owner could carry a tune.

The Nutcracker King did not like the prospect of rocking the night away. He had a feeling it wasn't going to be a swell time.

4

Christmas Eve rolled up like a revived steam locomotive that has discovered a new purpose in life. The party was set to start at 7pm and continue through to midnight, Christmas Day. Louis was dressed in his best tuxedo, bought for a bargain at a local charity shop. It gave him an authentic appearance as a host and allowed him to assume the role of referee if things got a little out of hand, which rarely happened as the majority of the people attending were true veterans to the fetish scene. The Nutcracker King was placed on a small podium positioned at the centre of the room.

It was time.

A group of five men and five women gathered inside the room and stared at the newfangled object on the podium. Most of them were easily in the 30 to 50 age range, none of them attractive enough to be considered prized catches, but a couple of the women could pass off as being decent looking human beings.

Louis spoke in a raised voice:

"Ladies and Gentlemen welcome to the third annual XXXmas Bash! I will kick off this year by welcoming a new addition to the Treasure Trove; you have probably already seen him there on that mini podium. I give you the Nutcracker King; a rare oddity from Iceland designed to efficiently crack any kind of nut you could possibly imagine with his strong Viking like jaws. Ladies, please feel free to use him on your submissive men, I know some of these guys love having their nuts cracked on Christmas Eve!"

Louis reached into the side pocket of his blazer and produced a silicone breast implant; he threw it on the floor with vigour and stamped on it like he was at a Jewish wedding, he even proclaimed the words: "Mazel Tov!" with outstretched arms and a great effulgent smile was smeared across his bearded face.

The Nutcracker King's soft inner organs filled with a ghastly understanding. He now knew his fate, and wished ever so hard that he was in the antique shop, nestled between the legs of those two porcelain dolls.

5

Our silent victim, the Nutcracker King was moved from his podium and onto a shelf that clung to the centre wall where he could survey in silent disbelief the rogues that intended to defame his dignity. For the first couple of hours it was a tame scene, far from gentle, but about as tame as you could get for an S&M party. In the background Yuletide songs made famous by infamous one hit wonder artists echoed throughout the scene as the players fondled and gyrated in their seductive foreplay. Couples kissed without locking mouths, just rolling their tongues together in primitive desperation like they were separated by an invisible wall and the only breach was a small hole big enough for their slimy rouge tongues.

The music ceased, the men and women were naked, revealing rolls of fat, caesarean scars, fading stretch marks, greying hairs, wrinkles, cellulite, browned genitalia, and breasts that had seen better days, on both genders.

Louis stood as if he were prepared to make a toast, he rasped his foot on the floor to gather attention, and when he had it he began to speak:

"Ladies and Gentlemen, now that you are all well acquainted with one another I think it is time for me to tell you my annual Christmas tale. For those of you who don't know; every year I regale you sexy folk in a piece of flash fiction I write about that year's festive season. This year I give you the tale of Santa and his Spunk Sleigh."

'In this modern day & age would Santa bother to use his trademark sleigh and flying reindeer? With all this technology: cameras, satellites and military protection, would Santa use something so primitive and so detectable? He has got to stay incognito right? Well, I know an indisputable fact and it may blow your minds to smithereens!

Santa has been working with a top-secret team of scientists, engineers and technicians at Area 51 to help him build the Spunk Sleigh '11. A stream lined stealth jet that uses warp drive technology to help him travel around the world in one night. The reindeers finally got that retirement cheque they've been waiting for! Why is it called the "Spunk Sleigh?" well as I can recall, Santa dropped into Area 51 one day in the summer of 2009 and said to the guys:

"I need a new sleigh, and it's got to have spunk!"

But that's not the only reason: the Spunk Sleigh has a tube embedded underneath the piloting stick that connects to Santa's fat jolly ole member. It twirls and pulses and sucks Santa off while he flies across the globe at supersonic speed, all this time he is stuck in perpetual ejaculation mode, you would think that all of those orgasms would kill a man, but Santa is a magical being with a never-ending supply of semen...how else did you think he got a fat belly? All of that glistening white spunk travels through the pipe and gets sprayed out of the exhaust at the rear end of the sleigh creating what appears to be snow. So on Christmas Day, when your children are playing in the snow making angels and constructing armies of snowmen, just remember that it's Santa's spunk they have smeared all over their faces!'

"Thank you!"

The folks in the room howled with laughter, cheered and slapped each other senseless. The Nutcracker King couldn't help but think it was a pile of ectoplasmic drivel not worthy of having any physical place in this world. He came to resent Louis at that moment; if it wasn't for that bearded dolt, he might have still been in Ancient Exposures smelling that porcelain pussy. But no, here he was trapped in a room with a bunch of bottom feeders who actually looked as though they were about to eat each other's bottoms for supper. Louis opened his fat disgraceful mouth again and spewed out more words:

"Thank you, thank you, I'm glad you all enjoyed. One day, when we've been doing this for a few more years I'll compile my tales into a book and give you all free copies as a memory; maybe something to tell the Grandkids. Anyway, enough of me, please continue!"

The fiasco did continue, and things delved into the deep waters of depravity very fast. A fat man climbed onto the sleigh bed and donned a tight pair of red PVC pants; he pulled on a fake bushy white beard complete with the red and white hat and posed as a haggard Santa Claus. Four naked women locked the spiked collars around their necks, attached to the leads like dogs, no… reindeers, because they even wore the antlers for that authentic Kris Kringle feel. Four other men clothed themselves in the garments of genuine North Pole Elves like they were ready for another day in Santa's nefarious workshop. The haggard Santa clutched a whip and started to give his reindeer whores a fierce lashing, they cried like humans and whinnied like real deer. They pulled until the leads were tight and pretended to drag the sleigh bed through an imaginary sky, flexing their bodies and sweating profusely. The elves unzipped and gave their hard cocks to the reindeer whores, controlling the movements by pulling their hair, forcing them to gag, a couple puked and buried their faces in the puddles while the elves slapped their faces and whacked their tits with brutal lust.

Then came the crux, the moment he had been waiting for but hoped would never come. The final woman, the one not involved in the odious orgy grabbed our Nutcracker King and introduced him to the deepest pit of hell; she forced open his mouth, gaping and unnaturally willing, and grabbed the scrotum of one of the elves and pushed his biggest testicle into the Nutcracker King's mouth.

Clamp.

He could taste salt, sweat, and hair tickling the roof of his mouth. If only he could speak, if only he could move, he would clamp down hard and tear the fleshy ball right off and make a run for the window. The elf screamed in a paradoxical cry of pain and pleasure, the Nutcracker King felt the testicle convulse and knew the man was ejaculating inside the reindeer whore's mouth, she swallowed and looked deviously into his eyes. This process was repeated on the other three elves with the same outcome. The Nutcracker King felt like his very soul had been defiled.

During this dramatic scene, Louis Thwaite was sat comfortably on the sofa reading a fantasy novel about a man on an obsessive quest to find a tower. This kind of role-play didn't interest him, sometimes he would masturbate during the normal gangbang moments, but it seemed his little tale about Santa had sparked something tribal in these people, so he left them to it and tried to chew through the 600-page novel.

The party began to wind down at around 11pm, both men and women had come enough times to fill a large paddling pool, especially if you added the amount of urine that had been excreted at the time. The mannequin was reduced to a broken pile of plastic limbs. The Nutcracker King was lost, he had been cast upon the floor in a puddle of someone's piss, used and most certainly abused. If only he could speak, if only he could move, he would cry uncontrollably and curl up in a ball underneath some dark place where no one could see his shame. His resentment boiled into a deep-rooted hatred for Louis Thwaite, here was a man with no conscience, no ability to empathise with a simple Nutcracker King. If only he could move, he would murder that bearded delinquent; he didn't need the ability to speak to do that.

Louis saw off the last of party attendees just before midnight, he didn't offer showers, just free packets of facial wipes and a few sprays of deodorant. It was a happy moment for him; not only had he made an exceptional amount of money, he would also be home in time for Christmas to get some Yuletide loving from Matilda. He would leave the room until Boxing Day. After all, who cleans up on the most festive day of the year?

6

The morning of December 27th Matilda Oswald woke up with an intrusive hangover and covered in bite marks. The floor was littered with used crackers and streams of exploded party poppers, not to mention the unhealthy amount of empty wine bottles and cans of lager and the odd bottle of single malt scotch. Christmas Day and Boxing Day were a blurred haze, a past now decaying in her mind. She felt no love in that sensitive state. Louis snored peacefully but she was damned if he wasn't going to suffer with her. Matilda nudged him awake.

Louis jolted up, snorting back a rock of snot and coughed erratically.

"Fuck, my head. What a year! Ugh, I need juice and the flesh of a dead animal."

Matilda smiled in satisfaction and got up to make breakfast. While she rummaged through the fridge for leftovers she heard Louis exclaim:

"Oh Christ on a cracker! The room, I forgot to clean out the damn room. Okay, okay, that's today's priority chore. Clean up the mess my clientele left. What a generous fucking gift."

The Nutcracker King had never felt so miserable, out of all the Christmases

he had experienced this was the most humiliating and depressing. He felt

like a copycat baboon whose master had died and left it alone in a cage with

nothing to imitate but its isolation and the corpse of its master.

The puddle of urine was dry and felt crusty against his stiff wooden body.

For two days he was a prisoner in that room, staring into endless dark,

Christmas Day had passed him by and he was pretty sure Boxing Day had

stumbled past trying to be inconspicuous, but failing miserably. He wasn't

sure he would ever escape, maybe Louis had consumed too much alcohol

and died of liver poisoning or threw himself off a bridge because of what he

had done to the Nutcracker King. Both theories were, of course, complete

nonsense. But he wouldn't mind spending an eternity in nothingness if he

knew that rotten bastard was dead.

When he saw Matilda's face he was delighted, she had come to rescue him

from torment. He saw no sign of Louis, later the Nutcracker King learned

that Matilda had struck a deal with her other half: if he cleaned their apartment and prepared dinner, she would tidy the party room. Her excuse was because she wanted some fresh air to help soothe the hangover that currently dominated the interior of her head. That was half of the truth; the other half was curiosity, to see what chaos these people left behind, to build a picture in her mind of the events preceding the damage. When she surveyed the aftermath her imagination refused to work, it was shocked into mental silence. It was infinitely worse off than their bedroom; it was like a boulder of sin had crashed through the shop leaving behind debauched debris in its wake. Midway through optically scanning she noticed something lying on the floor, something that seemed insignificant yet was unavoidable to miss. It was a nutcracker dressed in the regal garments of a king.

She picked it up, looked into its eyes and started turned it back and forth, examining the alluring toy. Matilda felt like it was seducing her, whispering in her ear like a ghost. The Nutcracker King stared back with indifference, paying no heed to her moistened eyes and full red lips, yet the soft inner cogs of her mind clicked and recognised an attraction. Matilda whispered:

"Fuck it, he'll never know," and stuffed the toy into her handbag. She felt awful inside, like she had betrayed Louis, but a wave of excitement crashed and drowned those doubts.

The Nutcracker King could not believe his luck; he was saved from certain doom. He owed everything to Matilda Oswald. If only he could speak, if only he could move, he would take her to a quaint log cabin in the woods, lay her down by the fire and thank her properly. His organic entrails purred with anticipation, it was a good omen indeed, signalling change and the possibility of a new destiny. One he hoped would bring him closer to the demise of Louis Thwaite.

7

When Matilda arrived back at the apartment there was no sign of Louis, the place was clean but her partner was nowhere to be seen. She took the nutcracker out of her bag and examined it again, it coldly seduced her and made something in her crotch twitch and the longer she stared the more unbearable it became. She threw the bag on the floor, got undressed and lay on the bed. Matilda began to gently push the nutcracker into her pussy, but something scratched and made her yelp in pain. It was the crown, too sharp; she would need to do some maintenance before continuing.

Matilda Oswald owned a craft shop in Aurum's Desire, not too far away from Follicly Endowed. Her place was called 'Matilda's Marvels,' and she sold various trinkets, household ornaments and collectors' toys. Sometimes she would have to restore certain items in her workshop if they were delivered damaged (she mostly worked on a donation basis). This was the place she took the Nutcracker King to perform some low-level maintenance. First, she trimmed off his fuzzy white hair and smoothed down his crown and shoulders to make him more streamlined. The Nutcracker King only felt the pain in his shoulders, but he didn't mind because he knew what would

be coming next. It was a beautiful kind of revenge, he certainly couldn't do

anything himself to harm Louis Thwaite, but his spouse was unknowingly

enacting the revenge. Nothing says 'fuck you, buddy' than violating a man's

other half. Matilda gave him a fresh lick of paint, thinking she might as well

go the whole hog since she had made the effort to go to the workshop. After

the paint was dry she brushed on a coat of varnish, stepped back and

admired her handy work. She had created something never before seen in

the world: a Nutcracker King Dildo. A sex toy designed to pleasure women,

but could also be used as a weapon to punish men.

When Matilda arrived back at the apartment Louis was still nowhere to be

seen. His lack of presence made her feel uneasy, yet somewhat aroused

since she could now create a taboo situation using her new sex toy. Repeat as

before: she dropped her bag and stripped off her clothes. The only thing

that wouldn't be repeated was the pain; this new aspect would be smooth

sailing. Once she was naked she made a nest upon the bed and once again

playfully slid the Nutcracker King inside her wet, tingling pussy. There were no snags and it went in with ease. Deep down Matilda felt filthy, wrongfully filthy, in a way she had never felt before.

The situation was so out of place and out of character, but nothing stepped in to cease these vile actions. Conscience and actions were working against one another to sow the seeds of a diminishing personality. Every step closer to orgasm was another step closer towards losing her grip on reality. Beat after beat and every thrust after thrust gradually pushed her towards that inexorable orgasm; it made her stomach cramp and her legs twitched feverishly. As she steadied her breathing and tried to gain more clarity from the colossal body shock, Matilda felt a vibrating sensation inside her accompanied by a sound that was halfway between a moan and a hum. When she pulled the Nutcracker King out of her cunt, she saw that its lips were pursed while it made a deep groaning sound. There was confusion mixed in with a brief state of denial. Of course, that all broke into terror when the thing finally spoke:

"I could die a happy man. The piquancy brought me such a pleasant rush, it was an untold experience, most of us keep that information to ourselves because to inform on our conscious mind would be a betrayal against the secret element that lurks within."

Matilda Oswald wanted to howl in horror, but she only grew more wet and desiring.

"The pleasures of the flesh outweigh the sins of the soul," she said in a hypnotic state, and inserted the Nutcracker King back inside her.

Somewhere, in the abyssal chambers of her subconscious, the soul of Matilda watched through a spherical window and cried. She had relinquished control to some unknown force. She was powerless, a prisoner caged inside her own mind.

She wished ever so hard that Louis had not come home with that dreadful nutcracker, it was to be the tool of their demise, and there was nothing she could do to stop it. She came to orgasm again.

8

"It has been such an awful long time since I last spoke," he coughed. The Nutcracker King's voice was creaky and occasionally dust spewed out of that abnormal mouth of his. "It is a barbaric way my people exile those who oppose the kingdom, although I did not oppose anything. I ruled like a king should, but I failed in winning the Vermin War and for that I was cast out. Listen to me, rambling like an old man with dementia. So much to do, so much to say, but so little time I have at this moment. Matilda my dear, you were mine from the moment I laid eyes upon you, and you will be mine whether you desire to be or not, for our destinies are entwined like serpents seducing the eyes of hungry spectators hoping for their luscious hallucinogenic venom. We will be together in front of the fire toasting the health of our entangled fate. There is but one problem: Louis Thwaite. That sleazy, deplorable excuse for a human must be eradicated from this existence. You will help me in this matter Matilda. It will seal our pact and join our souls in matrimony. A cocktail of two bloods merging."

Matilda nodded in agreement, though her face slightly twitched, it was a subtle expression of agony, the subconscious prisoner screamed out in anguish. They were still lying in the bed, her sweating chest heaving and lips full bodied with rouge smears. The Nutcracker King still appeared indifferent, but his eyes burned with a passion so fierce it could birth a new star. He was finally free from his exile, free to wander the Earth, to search for a door into his kingdom, and to claim back what was rightfully his. But he wouldn't, he had spent too long in silence, watching the world pass him by and not regard him. He was resentful of the human race, but now he was in love with one its people. Matilda was to be his Nutcracker Queen in a new kingdom with a population of only them. It was true that she was under a spell; he had cast it on her using up every morsel of telepathic energy he could muster and the hatred he felt for Louis gave him an extra boost. When she had looked into his blank, meaningless eyes back in the party room she was ensnared, and when her cunt miraculously brought him back to life, he was able to further tug the ropes of the mental net that engulfed her.

Matilda's facial features possessed a kind of blankness only a comatose patient would own, but her body and mind were still coming to terms with the hypnosis. Soon that miniscule resisting element within would accept this new state of being and give up, and then she would be fully consumed and become a new woman. His woman. Now he could speak, now he could move, and he was going to fulfil his promise of thanking her in that log cabin.

The sun began to set over the rolling hills of Aurum's Desire. Matilda put on her clothes and waited for Louis to arrive. The Nutcracker King was lying in wait under the bed, he was a wicked sprite poised to cause some horrific mischief. The monster you feared when falling asleep.

Louis was sat on a bench in the local park, he supped on a can of dandelion & burdock; a rare treat he allowed himself from time to time as it brought back fond, yet sad memories of his grandmother. He had spent the day shopping for groceries feeling like a primitive man hunting for food in the wild forests of our ancestors.

His plan was to construct a scrumptious meal for Matilda, to thank her for tidying the party room in the shop. Louis relished taking some time out in the park, it allowed him to flip reality's switch and tune into his thoughts.

Plans rushed through his mind. Maybe it was time to give up working in the sex shop industry.

If that industry even exists anymore. Thank you, internet.

He did enjoy the annual S&M parties and would probably carry on hosting them, perhaps in a more discreet manner. The business wasn't really bringing in much money, Matilda's Marvels had been supporting them for the past three years and his income was just a nice little top up. He wanted to change his attitudes and invest in something else, keep the shop but completely refurbish it into an establishment that would work well in a small town. Even Matilda said the name "Follicly Endowed" sounded like it belonged on the front doors of a beard specialist's studio.

The logistics could wait, the sun was setting, and it was time to start home. He planned to speak to Matilda about his plans over dinner; she had always been good to him and rarely complained about his financial situation. They loved one another; it was as simple as that.

The apartment was dimly lit when Louis entered. He threw his keys onto a small table next to the door and switched on the main light.

"Matilda, you here babe?" he asked the empty room.

"I'm in bed," she replied.

Something didn't sound right about the tone of her voice; it sounded empty, kind of deadpan. Maybe she was ill, they did have a gargantuan session over Christmas, which would explain why she didn't sound quite right.

He walked into the bedroom and saw his love lying on the bed naked and playing with herself, she writhed on the sheets causing them to crease and warp out of shape. Louis' eyes widened with delight.

"Now this is what I call a welcome," he said and began to get undressed down to his bare skin. He climbed on top of Matilda and started kissing her neck while caressing her breasts, pinching her nipples hard, loving the soft squeals she produced. She carried on touching herself, occasionally stroking his hard cock.

Louis contorted his body so he moved in unison with her, those teasing moments when she touched him drove him insane with pleasure, but it all ended as quickly as it begun. He felt a sharp pain on his cock, when he looked down it was bleeding; Matilda must have scratched it, but when he averted his attention onto her he saw she was holding a thin razorblade.

"Baby what the…" he looked into her eyes, the first time he had since entering the bedroom. What he saw was something dead, something hollow. Something missing.

"You're not my Matilda," he said and before he could jolt his body off she grabbed hold of his neck and squeezed with an alien strength. Louis blacked out.

9

His eyes opened gradually, feeling like they were made of solid plastic, and the world slowly melted into focus. Matilda stood over him, still naked, she was a looming presence that reminded him of nightmares he had when he was a child. She tied his arms to the bedposts using the handcuffs he once acquired from an ex-policeman at the inaugural annual Christmas orgy. Something flicked his big toe hard and he let out a high-pitched yelp, he almost passed out with fright when he saw the source of the flick. It was the Nutcracker King from the antique shop, though slightly misshaped. The toy was not an inanimate object anymore; it was a living and breathing creature that flashed an insidious smile at him.

"Hello Louis. I have met you but, you haven't properly met me yet, as I have been somewhat indisposed of late. I am the King of all Nutcrackers. *The* Nutcracker King and I will be the last thing you see on this wretched world." He produced two silver bells and attached one on each of Louis' big toes. "I call these the slay bells, hear them go ring ding dinga ding doo, for it is lovely weather for a slay ride together with you. Whatever is the matter with you dear boy? Your face looks like you've just seen an orphanage burn to the ground."

When the Nutcracker King laughed it sounded like rats gnawing on wood.

Louis opened his mouth to shriek in terror but before a sound could escape, Matilda shoved a filthy sock in his gob. He shot a pained look at her and saw his lover's face twitch, she was sobbing inside, Louis could tell. She grabbed hold of his cock and started stroking. He had never felt so vulnerable, because considering the bizarre situation he still hardened in a state of arousal. While he was being pleasured, the Nutcracker King approached his crotch area with a creepy stiffness that looked like he was marching. Louis was beginning to drift off and lose himself, maybe he was sleeping on that park bench and all of this was a dream. If only he could move, he would pinch himself to wake up. There was no need, though. Just before he could ejaculate, he felt something explode in his right testicle. He howled, the sock muffling the sound. When he looked down, he saw great blobs of maroon gushing from where his right testicle had been, and there was the Nutcracker King with something fleshy protruding from his mouth. He spat it onto the sheets and spoke:

"Oh Mr. Thwaite, it is a terrible ordeal when you cannot move or be heard when being put through such a torturing experience. I would feel so sad for you, but it is only what you deserve for being such a perverse creature."

The demon's mouth dropped open; Louis sobbed uncontrollably, shaking his head in a begging gesture. He desperately wanted mercy. The Nutcracker King filled his mouth with Louis' left testicle, the larger one, and clamped down with all his might. The small fleshy globe imploded and produced a burst of warm satisfying liquid. The Nutcracker King allowed his face to be covered with blood and listened with pleasure to the muffled cries of the restrained man.

Louis' body convulsed, adrenaline flowed through him and he fiercely thrashed to try and escape his bonds. It was a futile endeavour. All hope was lost. Matilda's face was expressionless, but that didn't stop her eyes from glistening with tears. He knew she was in there, somewhere, deep down being forced to watch all of this. He wished he had never gone to that damned antique shop, he wished that he would wake up the day after Boxing Day and realise it was all just an intoxicated dream. He wished a lot of things in that delirious moment of pain and horror. Matilda had not stopped stroking his cock and once the pain had numbed he grew hard

again, something he thought would be impossible, but when a wooden

Nutcracker King could walk, talk and bite off your balls he supposed

anything was possible. Matilda climbed on top of Louis, straddling him, and

slid his cock inside her sopping wet pussy. She rode him angrily and grinded

so deep that it hurt her inside, she punished herself and punished him.

There had been a kitchen knife lying on the bedside table, something she

had prepared earlier for this moment. Matilda grabbed the knife and

slammed it into Louis' neck and began to hack away at his flesh like a

possessed butcher. The Nutcracker King climbed onto Louis' chest and

looked into his eyes.

"You took away my Christmas and my dignity, so I am repaying you by

taking your life. Happy Holidays," he said, smiling that insidious smile.

Matilda watched the life leave her partner's eyes and blood spurted in every

direction. The subconscious prisoner crawled into a pocket of darkness and

cried manically. Louis Thwaite was dead and the Nutcracker King felt a

tsunami of satisfaction wash through his soul.

He turned to Matilda once she relinquished the knife:

"Thank you my dear, now we are bound together, our bloods intertwined creating an undying thirst for love. Your first act as my spouse will be something simple. I didn't have a Christmas this year and would very much appreciate it if you could rectify this. I have already had my Christmas wish, but now I would like my Christmas feast."

Epilogue

Sickly Christmas music echoed throughout the apartment and operatic singing accompanied the tunes, it has been so long since he last performed melodies. He sipped on a glass of sherry, a wonderful Yuletide tradition. The alcohol flowed through his small body and unleashed a fresh essence inside of him, he was not a stranger to the intoxicating liquid, but they had been estranged for oh so long.

"I wish it could be Christmas every day," he whispered in tune to the warming gas fire. It was no log fire, but he intended to make love in front of it all the same. From the kitchen the Nutcracker King could hear his new wife preparing the feast; it was to be a Christmas dinner unlike no other, a meal that literally had all the trimmings. He heard her sniff, as if she were crying, but he assumed she was chopping the onions; those blighters could be real buggers on the old tear ducts.

The Nutcracker King surveyed his new kingdom and was pleased with what he had achieved. If only his people could see him now, they would beg him to return and be their liege again, and he would return, but only to burn his old kingdom to the ground.

Matilda stood in the kitchen and prepared her King's feast like she was running on robotic autopilot. She was indeed chopping something, but they were not onions. On the marble kitchen surface she casually chopped the fingers from Louis' severed hand and laid them out on a baking tray, then coating them with a honey and whisky glaze. The digits sat between several parsnips and were waiting to be roasted. The main task was the most difficult for her soul. Lying upon the dinner table there was a great slab of meat. It was the torso of Louis Thwaite, she had severed the arms and legs to the point where it would fit in the oven, and the rectum still remained. She basted the flesh with melted butter infused with herbs. She had prepared a mean stuffing made from a blend of sage, onion, bacon and Louis' liver. Matilda took great handfuls of the stuffing and shoved it deep into the cavity of his torso via the sphincter. Tears rolled down her expressionless face, though the twitches had stopped because the subconscious prisoner was starting to relinquish all hope, she still cowered in the dark corner of that abstract cell and tried to swat away the taunting flies;

they were memories of the man she once loved, coming back to haunt her either in an attempt to comfort, or an attempt to mock and tell her she could have done more. That she was an imbecile for letting her guard down, but it could not be helped, she was doomed from the beginning. They both were.

When Matilda and the Nutcracker King had consumed the feast they both took a seat in front of the gas fire. Each of them had a glass of sherry and a mince pie, the final part of that age old Christmas tradition. The Nutcracker King proposed a toast to the health of their entangled fate and tapped his glass against hers, savouring the sweet chime.

"Merry Christmas, Matilda."

She stared longingly, eyes almost penetrating his wooden exterior, the dried tracks of her tears stood out against the makeup. In the end she slowly released a confident smile that radiated the Nutcracker King's world.

"Merry Christmas," she said to her new love.

The End

PANTOMIME OF HORRORS

Prologue

There were maggots in his advent calendar. They were disgusting, writhing creatures that gnawed at the cardboard in the 24th window. He struggled to keep his breakfast down, knowing he would only belch out coffee, toast, and bile. The wallpaper peeled and beetles scurried around the Christmas tree, they made a sickening noise, like sharp fingernails scratching on sandpaper. He felt dizzy. The maggots dropped out of the little window and onto the coffee table, each one screeched as if in pain, he tried to thwart the hideous sounds by covering his ears. The noises were inside his head, infesting his brain. He could almost feel the maggots chewing away at his thoughts. A song about sleigh bells ringing blared from the television and the angel on top of the tree winked sadistically.

He cried.

He had brought this all upon himself, now he was paying the price only a damned man could afford. Ants crawled on the carpet and formed the shapes of snowflakes and transformed them into snowmen with twisted smiles.

That confounded suit.

He wished he had never applied for that Christmas vacancy, he wished he had just walked on by and let it pass from his memory, but the desperation for a job and money got the better of him.

Now it wanted him.

That creature he thought only existed in films and grim tales of monsters. It was causing all this chaos, preparing his state of mind for a horrifying journey. At that moment a man who sang festively about giving his heart away on Christmas day replaced the jingle about sleigh bells.

On the television he saw not the original music video, but another. In this version the 80s singer stabbed himself in the chest, ripped out his own beating heart and offered it to Santa. On his knees the singer smiled and breathed heavily, blood dripping through his fingers. Santa took the heart and ate it in one agonising mouthful. He smacked his lips together in satisfaction and laughed in his signature '*Ho, Ho, Ho!*' manner. Then it happened, the unspeakable horror, the one that almost tipped him over the edge of sanity, plunging him deep into the well of madness. The red and white figure on the television turned its head, moving like a wooden doll, the

185

screen glitched and the static maggots briefly appeared, then Santa, that jolly old bastard from the Coke adverts smiled directly at him. It was not a jolly smile like you would imagine, it was a smile full of malice and with each glitch it transformed into something horrific, something you would only see in your darkest nightmares. Tainted pale skin leaked onto Santa's face, like a thick layer of make-up, the teeth yellowed and became like chunks of discoloured ivory, and the eyes burned with ferocity and became something reptilian. It was an impish face and it had long flowing dark hair with a single golden streak running through its fringe. He wanted to look, and he desperately wanted to look away, he wanted to see what this foul thing would look like, but he wanted to snatch his gaze away from that box and run outside in the snow. He wanted to make snow angels and die from hypothermia.

He wanted to die.

Anything but look that that horrible creature on the television.

The sinister Saint Nick sang his own creepy interpretation of the song on the television:

"Once bitten and always mine, you keep your distance, but I'll still eat you alive, tell me, Carson, do you recognize me? Well, I wouldn't worry, you'll soon get to know me. Merry Christmas, I wrapped you up inside me, with the notion that you'll never be free, I mean it. Now you know where it all begins, but if you kiss me now it will be your grisly end."

Santa's smile widened and it almost consumed his face. Santa laughed. It was a laugh that sounded like a thousand dying children. It reached for him through the television, breaking the walls of reality.

He screamed, he wailed for his sweet dear life and before his voice could become raw, before the monster could grab his face and peel his skin.

It stopped.

Normality was restored.

1

He almost tripped on the pavement. The damn slabs had been disrupted by road works and the fact he was more than mildly intoxicated did not help. There were mixed aromas in the air, curry sauce and frying fish wafted through the dark alleyway, the fish and chip shop was closing after a late-night rush. It was difficult to perceive the world around him. A single streetlamp cast a dim amber light upon the centre of the alley a few feet down, but it was enough for him to perceive the poster attached to the side of the chip shop. He pulled it off and held it in his hands:

SPREAD CHRISTMAS CHEER THIS YEAR!

Job Vacancies

At

Carmen's Curiosity Emporium!

Be the one and only

Jolly Ole Saint Nick!

Below there was a contact number and a name: Tanya Tatton and the location: The Red King Shopping Centre. He licked his lips and stuffed the poster in his coat pocket.

Carson Elwin had been on the unemployment line for over a year, times were becoming increasingly desperate as the months rolled by. More recently he has had to put his dreams of being a career writer on hold, in order to focus his time on finding some form of paid work. Something told him fate had intervened at that moment, and though it did not sound like a glamorous job, he knew that if he was successful in his application maybe Christmas would not be so lousy this year.

He ran the rest of way home, his feet splashing in fresh puddles as he went and the cold water seeped through his canvas shoes. His blood pumped through his veins and warmed his body to an uncomfortable temperature, sweat spasmed on his forehead then evaporated in a chilly haze. At 3am during the winter the temperature plummeted to unbearable levels in the town of Secular, but something felt different about this cold; something bitter was trying to gouge its way through his beer coat and nibble at his fragile human skin.

2

The next day he awoke early in order to acquire an application form, at least that is what he assumed he would be garnering from calling them.

"Good morning, Carmen's Curiosity Emporium, Tanya speaking, how can I help?" she sounded cheerful and ready to aid in his enquiry.

"Oh, hello, I came across your advertisement last night, for the job vacancy at your establishment. Is it possible to collect an application form from you please, or would it have to be sent in the post?" he sounded nervous, not a good sign.

"Oh that's wonderful! I am delighted to hear of your interest for this position. Do you have a curriculum vitae?"

"As a matter of fact I do."

"Wonderful, are you free this afternoon, say around 1pm?"

"Yes I am."

"Splendid! Come in at 1pm and we will interview you."

Carson was taken aback, he never expected things to move this fast. He shook himself out of the shock and replied, trying to sound nonchalant.

"That sounds perfect. See you at one."

"Could I have your name please?"

"Carson Elwin."

"Wonderful Carson, I have pencilled you in for a one o'clock engagement. Goodbye."

"Bye!"

He stood in silence for a few minutes, flabbergasted by the swift response to his simple enquiry; he then began the process of tidying himself up for the interview.

Carmen's Curiosity Emporium was not the small store he had been expecting, on the contrary it was a rather expansive shop filled with various gadgets and antiques, a curious cocktail of antiquities and modern technological items. At the centre of the shop were a series of miniature festive stalls, they looked like the kind of log cabins you would find at a Christmas market and sold all kinds of Christmas themed goods. All around him he could hear Yuletide pop music filling his ears - some guy was telling him how he wished it could be Christmas every day, but Carson did not share this sentiment. He shivered, like he had been hit by a colossal icy gust and was overwhelmed by a sense of impending dread, but he chalked this up to pre-interview nerves.

A tall slender lady approached him; she was dressed in smart attire consisting of a dark grey pencil skirt, white shirt and a dark grey blazer. She would have been intimidating if not for the ridiculous Santa hat resting on her head; on the bobble was a small golden bell that tinkled with every step she took. The slender lady peered at him through box-rimmed glasses that added an almost geeky quality to her outfit; she smiled and extended her hand.

"You must be Carson. I'm Tanya," she said.

He took her soft hand in his and shook.

"I am. How did you guess?"

"Well, the fact you are wearing a dashing suit is a dead giveaway," she giggled like a schoolgirl, her attempt to diffuse his nerves did not work, it only served to make him more anxious. His suit was not dashing either and would not be classed as a real suit, he wore black skinny jeans in place of trousers and was only clothed in a white shirt with no tie and black suit jacket, but he had a presentable appearance; smelling fresh and looking clean, and so far it seemed to impress her. Unless, of course, she was being sarcastic.

They sat in a small office. Tanya took his curriculum vitae and spent a couple of minutes pouring her attention over it, her brow was furrowed in concentration and after that awkward silence between the two of them, she looked up and smiled, showing off her pearly white teeth, and sat in a more comfortable manner in her leather chair.

"So, Carson Elwin, why do you want to work here?"

3

The phone rang.

"Hello?"

"Hey Dad, I've got some news. I've got a job!" said Carson.

His father bellowed a joyful noise over the phone.

"Terrific news Son! What will you be doing?"

"Nothing glamorous, I'll be working in that curiosity shop at the Red King Shopping Centre, my role will involve me dressing up as jolly ole Saint Nick."

This sentence was followed by an uproar of laughter over the phone line.

His father said: "So you will be donning the festive cheer complete with beard and hat then?"

"Not quite, see that's what I thought would happen, but instead I will be dressing in one of those mascot outfits, like a full body suit complete with an oversized Santa Clause head mask. Like I said, nothing glamorous, but at least I can get some money ready for Christmas and New Year, it's a weekly paid position, which really helps. They want me to start tomorrow, the woman who interviewed me, she's the manager, said they wanted the

position filled last month but no one showed any interest in the vacancy.

Now that Christmas is approaching fast they need me to start immediately."

  "I guess you could say fate intervened. I'm happy for you Son, your Mother

will be too. Are you still coming home on Christmas Eve?"

  "Of course I am, won't be until the evening though as I will be working, but

you will see me. How was the show last night?"

  "Terrific! And the show went down a treat! The guys and dykes loved every

minute."

Carson's father, Gordon Elwin, worked part time as a drag queen in the

local gay bar during those late-night hours, when decent folk are probably

tucked up in bed ready to sweep that day beneath the carpet of the past. His

alter ego Valerie La Femme was a local celebrity and adored by the gay

community, as well as secretly desired by the straight. During the Christmas

period he performs his own rendition of the pantomime *Aladdin*, which he

calls *A Lad in My Lamp*, and like a pantomime he performs the show on

multiple nights with a cast of colourfully camp characters. This has earned

him the affectionate and apt nickname 'The Dame' from his peers. The crux of the show is when Valerie inserts a golden lamp into her anus and farts inside it, when she removes it plumes of fire erupt from the lamp's lid and smoke appears on stage along with an incredibly flamboyant and very attractive genie. It is at this point Valerie wishes for everyone in her audience to have a shot of Sambuca, this is granted by the manager and everyone roars with delight.

Carson bid his father farewell and wished him all the best for the remainder of his shows.

"And send Mother my love," he said.

"I will Son, she's in the basement at the moment but I'm sure she will pop up soon, I'm cooking dinner tonight so that will give her some reason to pry herself away from her alchemy."

"Bye Dad."

"Bye Carson."

4

It took three hours for him to slip into a satisfactory sleep; his mind had been troubled by something, but he could not place his finger on exactly what was troubling him. There were moments when his mind would settle and he thought sleep would take him, then that flame would ignite behind his closed eyes and the idea of sleep would dissipate and become an impossible wish. After the first hour he grew intensely frustrated and repeatedly punched his pillow, silently cursing through clenched teeth. After the second hour he felt like crying, loud voices chattered in his head, a hall of moving mouths uttering nonsensical words. Approaching the third hour he started to settle again, but background inner static still lingered and the sleep was shallow. Carson heard a rustle, he opened his eyes and sat up, staring at the darkness, he heard it again, a sort of rustling noise. The hairs on his arms stood on end and a lurid chill flowed through his body like cold hands running down his flesh. The rustle turned into what sounded like a slither.

"Hello?" he said, a stupid thing to ask considering no one was in the room. But the darkness was solid black, his curtains were open and usually a soft light from the street lamps outside would permeate through his window. There was no light, only blackness, it was as if a giant squid had spewed ink all over his walls. Carson began to shake, he felt ridiculous, a grown man being afraid of the dark, but instinct dictated otherwise. The slithering ceased and suddenly there was silence and sound of his heavy breathing. Minutes passed and before he could shake off his nerves something crackled, a flame ignited...

5

His eyes opened only to be greeted by blinding sunlight pouring through his window. His clock told him it was almost 8am and his brain told him to rehydrate or else he would shrivel into a pathetic prune. Carson did not give any thought to his nightmare; as far as he was concerned a mixture of nerves, excitement and frustration had triggered it. The quicker he forgot about it the better.

Easier said than done.

He drank a coffee that was strong enough to give a child cardiac arrest and prepared himself for his first day at work.

Slipping into his costume was a rather tedious affair that took longer than was necessary. The suit, when worn, was droll and looked as if it belonged in a garden centre with other inanimate Christmas statues, it was traditional and looked somewhat like a waxwork model. The head mask had an eerily realistic appearance, it came complete with glass eyes of which Carson assumed he would be able to see through, and he was correct. The mask possessed a lot of weight and he felt uncomfortable for a while, the world was a distorted mess when peering through those glass eyes, but it was

manageable and he had been told the majority of his day would be spent

seated on his festive throne waving to children and parents.

Inside the suit he felt a slight shock, like he had been touched by electricity,

but instead of jolting his flesh pimpled and waves of euphoric arousal flowed

through his body. It made him feel peculiar, it was the kind of weird and

wrong sensation one would get from masturbating over incestuous

pornography.

Time slowly and stubbornly desquamated like a cluster of warts. Upon his

festive throne, Carson stewed inside his suit and began to realise why the job

vacancy had not been snapped up by anyone else. He performed the usual

spiel to the children; their faces were a mixture of confused horror and

absolute joy at seeing their annual jolly hero, that morbidly obese bringer of

material possessions. Despite the claustrophobic confines of the costume, he

could still hear the world around him with great clarity, and so too could his

audience hear him when he proclaimed:

"Ho, ho, ho! Merry Christmas boys and girls!"

From the speakers in the shop came one of Carson's favourite Yuletide songs, it was performed by a ragtag group of Irish musicians and was about a bitter couple reminiscing on their love life.

 Being paid for lounging around and entertaining over-excited children was not as bad as he imagined. That was, until the weirdness started.

A curious sensation befell him and Carson could have sworn something had stroked his leg, not on the outside, but inside the suit. He trembled and felt his brow perspiring; suddenly the music wavered then sounded like it was being played in reverse. A voice spoke from within the suit:

 "I can see a better time where I make all of your dreams come true. I will take your cold hand in mine on Christmas Eve and promise you a fairytale in which we sing a lullaby and I steal those dreams. I've got a feeling, this year is for me and you."

Carson felt woozy and he began to shake, he tried to maintain his demeanour but it was a futile effort. He rose from his throne abruptly and exited the shop floor; once he was clear of the prying eyes of customers he ripped off the mask and forced his way into the lavatory.

His guts unfurled from his mouth in the form of half-digested food and coffee, he wretched and produced more putrid bile and his body quivered inside the sweltering suit. He was glad to have escaped that wretched mask though.

What had he experienced? Was he delirious from the intense heat inside the costume? Or had he suffered a psychotic break? Perhaps the illness that afflicted his mother was now beginning to take hold of him.

He apologised to Tanya profusely, she responded with compassion and told him to take a break until he had regained his composure. Carson liked her and found himself becoming somewhat attracted to her, but he knew his attraction would only extend as far as fantasy, even if she were not his boss, what would a professional career woman want with a lousy struggling writer who could not even find a decent job, let alone a realistic career? Carson was not an unattractive man, he had no problem finding women who wanted to share his bed for a night or two, but when it came to relationships attraction only went so far, and he knew he did not have the correct ingredients to be a partner to anyone. That is what he thought. His long tenure at Unemployment Central had caused a severe drop in his confidence and ofttimes he felt being alone was the most sensible thing he could do, until he got his life back on track at least.

 Once the nausea had faded, Carson got back into character and went to greet his delighted audience, he apologised to the children and their parents and explained that his reindeer were due to be fed their daily meal of carrots and hoped no one would question him.

6

The uneasy feeling that had stricken him at work still lingered when he arrived home. His stomach tumbled like a washing machine filled with tripe and he spent the majority of his evening sat in his studio apartment reflecting upon the voice he heard inside his suit. Carson contemplated his mental health and hoped his mind was not beginning to stir the same illness that affected his mother.

Sandra Elwin was, what many would consider, a religious fanatic. To others she was what Carson's circle of friends jokingly called 'bat shit crazy.' Sandra had a bizarre belief system, she believed in the existence of fairies and that they were the evolutionary relatives of dinosaurs and dominated the planet until humans were conceived. While some dinosaurs evolved into birds, certain smaller members of that ancient species developed intelligence and evolved into these tiny mythical beings. When humans began to grasp a foothold on the developmental ladder, they began to bring about the extinction of the fairies. Sandra saw herself as the leader of an underground cult whose goal was to create a potion in order to transform herself into the

God of Fairies, and when this metamorphosis was complete the fairies would return and reclaim the world as their own, so that humanity might know the true meaning of judgement. She spent most of her days locked away in the family basement dabbling in alchemy: needless to say her attempts were fruitless and this would often entice her into having a complete breakdown. It had been a burden on the household for many years, but Carson remembers his father telling him she had not always been like this. It had happened shortly after she given birth to their second child, their dead second child. Gordon could not bring himself to have the love of his life committed to an asylum, and while she was not a danger to herself or others he looked after her.

His performances as 'The Dame' were his recreational time, a way to escape his identity for a couple of hours and forget the stress of his tragic existence. Carson always wondered if her condition was a result of the stillbirth, or if it had always been there, locked away in his mother's subconscious and the stillbirth had just emancipated the insanity, like Pandora's Box. If the latter was the case, then would that mean it was a genetic condition? Carson had always hoped not, but after today he started to question his theory.

Once again sleep did not come easy, he flung around in his bed and could not decide if he was too warm beneath his duvet, but taking it off proved too cold for him to handle. He settled eventually and felt like he was ready to drift away, then it started again, the slithering sound he had heard the night before. Carson's eyes shot open and his body began to tremor with anxiety, like a frightened child he pulled the duvet over his head as if it would shield away any evil that lurked in the darkness. The slithering continued; it sounded like some creature was clambering over things in his room. He heard soft bumps and occasional bangs and he closed his eyes tight.

It must be a dream. I fell asleep. It's a night terror. I'll be fine.

But it felt all too real.

The commotion ceased and silence befell his room of rest. Carson slowly removed the bed sheets and sat up in his bed, he thought he saw something in the blackness. He rubbed his face in frustration, groaned and turned on the light.

What he saw made him howl in terror. His father was hanging from the ceiling by his arms and legs, thick metal hooks were embedded in his flesh and he dangled like a piece of meat in a butcher's shop. He was semiconscious and naked apart from his overly flamboyant makeup and luxurious purple wig.

"Dad?" said Carson. It was all he could manage through the tears.

A voice rose from the abyss:

"Ho. Ho. Ho."

Then it appeared, the Santa costume he had worn at work, it sprang up at the end of his bed and startled Carson, causing him to let out another terrified noise, only this time it was a high-pitched squeal, like a child who had just seen his pet being brutally squashed by a car. Santa moved towards Gordon, the monster's hands were covered in razor sharp claws, which it used to split open its victim's stomach. Gordon' innards exploded from the wound, blood gushed out like a pressurised barrel being ruptured by an axe. He did not make any sound of protest.

Carson watched Santa grab hold of his father's intestines, it started to move its gruesome hands up and down, masturbating the organ, it moaned with fierce sexual gratification, and Gordon followed suit. Carson was paralyzed, unable to aid his father in his time of need. But what could he do against such a demonic entity? His father's cock was stiff and throbbed, moving up and down as it twitched. As Gordon ejaculated, so too did his intestines, the snake like organ produced its own vile brown jizzom made of excrement and it squeezed out like icing from a funnel. The Santa costume lapped up this fetid waste like was sweet cream.

"I saw your mummy kissing Santa Claus, underneath the mistletoe, he ate her face and threw her corpse to the crows," said Gordon.

Santa turned to Carson and warped its wax-like face into what he thought was a smile. It spoke to him; it spoke through his soul and touched a place in his heart that only true monsters can touch.

"I see you when you're sleeping, I love the way you taste, I know when you are bad or good but I'm watching you, boy every day. With little sharp horns I'm coming for you, with little sharp teeth I'll chew and chew. With your fragile mind I'm going to play and I'll be filling my belly on Christmas Day."

Carson was beginning to grow weary of these confounded dreams, he awoke with a sticky face and fresh tears erupted from his eyes, he panicked and grasped his phone, dialling his father's number. Gordon assured his son the family was fine and followed that by informing Carson that both he and Mum would be making an appearance at his place of work to show their son some support. Carson groaned at his father's eagerness to see his son donning a full Santa Clause mascot costume.

Christmas was fast approaching and Carmen's Curiosity Emporium was positively heaving with enthusiastic children and a concoction of agitated parents and overly happy parents. A more traditional festive playlist pulsed through the speakers that day, a brass band performed a rendition of Good King Wenceslas and Carson felt more at ease once he had absorbed the convivial vibrations. In the staffroom toilets, he bathed his face in cold water and prepared himself for another day in the Santa suit. Waves of insecurity flowed through his body when adorning himself in that bewildering garb, and once again he was touched by mild electricity, this time the arousal he felt was almost exquisite, like feeling a woman's touch for the first time after being lost at sea. The festive throne was comfortable, that much he was thankful for. The day waned with each proclamation he made about Christmas being around the corner, that Santa would be checking his list, keeping an eye on all children.

"Who is naughty, who is nice? I'll check it once, I'll check it twice! Santa's coming down and I hope I will find peace on this Earth and goodwill to all mankind!" Carson sang to his audience, they cheered and laughed, the children's faces brightened as they smiled. He was overjoyed to hear their praise and settled in the suit, letting his guard down. He saw Tanya patrolling the shop floor, he gazed at her through those glassy eyes, and she beamed at him and threw him a thumb up.

It was mid-afternoon when his mother and father arrived, they perused the shop for a little while, browsing the peculiar wares on offer, when they saw their son they could not contain themselves, they waved excitedly, glowing with gleeful expressions. The combined warmth they exuded reminded Carson of a roaring log fire. It touched him emotionally to see his mother out of that damned basement and interacting with the real world, and to see

her smile too. He had not seen her smile for a long time. He wondered what

had changed.

Time decelerated and the movement of people's limbs looked like a canvas

of melting paint. Carson felt an invisible tentacle stroke his leg and he

started to perspire, feelings of deja vu made him feel nauseous. The world

became a hellish caricature filled with snow children painted with sinister

charcoal smiles and his parents were encased in sapphire ice coffins. The

invisible tentacle seductively found its way up his body, he froze in fright

and suddenly the costume became an expansive black space, the glassy eyes

drew further into a distance of nothingness, slowly becoming small glassy

orbs, where the world beyond continued to morph like warm plasticine.

Carson was flung into a state of shock when the tentacle began to grope his

crotch with lackadaisical movement. It was dreamlike, blurred and hazy,

with inaccessible audio ambiance. His manhood swelled and throbbed,

growing stiff with each stroking motion, he felt ashamed for garnering

pleasure from this heinous action, but he felt hypnotised, it seemed his

normal bodily reactions were rendered impotent, except for his cock. His mind was incapable of dredging up anti-sexual thoughts to distract him from the taboo actions being performed on him. A wet slime coated his cock and it felt as though an invisible cunt had squeezed him into a tight forbidden hole. It moved. Oh God it moved. It moved deliberate rocking motions, grinding, gyrating, goading his penis into bulging bigger. Tears tracked down his face, though he did not weep, instead he sighed in ecstasy and even moved his hips with this invisible sexual entity. Something tried to chew through the walls of his conscious mind, something was trying to tell him there was a world full of children and his parents out there, they were probably asking: Why is Santa moving in such a weird way Mummy? Daddy why does Santa sound like that? His parents were probably beside themselves, his mother's sunny disposition shattered, driving her back into the basement to torture her mind. All these thoughts trying to fiercely break through, yet he remained locked in that hypnotic state, puzzled by his lust and jerking spasmodically. A strange female voice sang tenderly in his ear:

"Good King Santa Claus looked out, on the Feast of Carson, when the snow lay round about, his buried corpse so even, brightly shone the Moon that night, my mouth devoured so cruel, when your poor flesh came in my sight, you became my winter fuel."

 The song made him tingle and he groaned loudly as he pushed his length deeper in the invisible entity.

 The world clumsily dissolved back into focus, the darkness diminished and Carson felt his member rupture with a violent orgasm. The melody of cheering children was no longer a distant ambiance; it was a shockingly intense barrage of clapping hands and joyous yells. According to the faces of his audience members it seemed he had been behaving as normal, running on autopilot while some mysterious force carried his mind off to a faraway world. He shook his head, perplexed by the sudden transition and Carson continued spreading Santa's Christmas joy to the customers of Carmen's Curiosity Emporium.

8

The weather outside was frightful, and Carson walked through a winter land filled with rampant consumers desperate to purchase last minute gifts. He bought a gingerbread latte from a local specialty coffee shop to help protect him against the furious frost that tainted the air. It had been snowing something fierce while he had been at work and the world was a sparkling white. Blankets of snow on the ground looked like frozen stars amongst the dense collection of flakes. Carson saw his breath escape via his mouth in immense white plumes, car exhausts belched out these same flourishes, but their toxins were something he could not admire. He came to a crossing by a roundabout the locals called 'The Bullring', almost slipping on the ice as he stared at that small island. Carson cried out in horror. At the centre of the Bullring was a huge Christmas tree, decorated with a vast trail of lights; the council did not put much effort into bedecking this tree, as it would, on occasions, be vandalised by drunk teenagers. It appeared to Carson that someone, or something, had decided to give the tree an angel. He saw severed limbs dangling from its branches, limbs of various ethnicities, fresh blood dripped from the wounds. Tinsel made of human entrails were intertwined with the fairy lights and crisscrossed around the fine fir tree, rouge plasma smeared the greenery. As his eyes scanned this macabre Yule-tree he began to fill with a colossal sense of dread. When his eyes reached the peak he could not help but scream, he could not help but cry in pathetic misery. At the tree's steeple he saw the Christmas Angel: his mother. Her disembowelled cadaver reigned supreme at the top, giant artificial wings had been sewn onto her back and all her corpse had been spattered with glistening glitter. Carson clutched his head with intense ferocity and felt his sanity steadily slipping from his grasp.

The angel's head turned to him, creaking as it did so, and the disfigured corpse of Sandra Elwin started to sing a Christmas carol to her crestfallen son:

"Silent night, your final night, you can't stay calm, you'll die in fright, your saviour's come to have his fill, it's no good running, just stay still. Sleep in heavenly peace, sleep in hellish peace."

A hand touched his shoulder, Carson whirled around and raised his fist and he saw a frightened and concerned old lady staring back at him.

"Steady dear, steady, what is the matter? You just started crying," she said.

Carson wiped his face and felt the moisture, he embraced the lady, who cried out in surprise. When she realised that he was not going to hurt her, she reciprocated the embrace.

"I think I'm losing my mind," he said as fresh bouts of tears burst through his eyes. The lady tenderly rubbed his back.

"I know that feeling dear. Do you have family?" she said.

"Yes, though I don't live with them, I was due to go and visit them on Christmas Eve."

"Well it's only a couple of days away, but I say go to them now, it's not healthy for a young man in your state to be alone this time of year. Go to them and strengthen your mind."

Carson released her from the embrace and smiled.

"Thank you," he said, and made his way home.

He spent the next two days at home with his parents; in those two days he had no incidents, meaning no psychotic breaks and no hallucinations. Maybe the old lady was right, he just needed some company. He aided his dad in those evenings, helping him choose outfits for his shows and straightening his wigs.

His mum seemed to be improving greatly, her behaviour was less erratic and she seemed to be spending less time in the basement. Carson knew it was the calm before another storm in her mind, but he hoped it would remain for a while.

He hoped even harder that she would just get better, he wanted to fix her, but she was irreparably damaged and he had to accept that fact.

Christmas Eve arrived with more snow flurries and Carson roused from a dreamless slumber, he felt good, mentally healthy and for the first time, excited about Christmas.

He felt festive.

9

Carson popped open his advent calendar and all of those feelings of merriment faded away; instead, his heart brimmed with dismay. There were maggots in his advent calendar. They were disgusting, writhing creatures that gnawed at the cardboard in the 24th window. He struggled to keep his breakfast down, knowing he would only spew out coffee, toast, and bile. The wallpaper peeled and beetles scurried around his father's perfectly decorated contemporary Christmas tree, they made a sickening noise, like sharp fingernails scratching on sandpaper. He felt dizzy.

The maggots dropped out of the little window and onto the coffee table, each one screeched as if in pain, he covered his ears to block out the hideous noises, but it was no good. The noises were inside his head, infesting his brain. He could almost feel the maggots chewing away at his thoughts.

A song about sleigh bells ringing blared from the television and the angel on top of the tree winked sadistically. Carson was reminded of his hallucination in town the other day, of his mother's mangled corpse hanging from the top of that horrific tree.

He cried.

He had brought this all upon himself, now he was paying the price only a damned man could afford. Ants crawled on the carpet and formed the shapes of snowflakes and transformed them into snowmen with twisted smiles.

That confounded suit.

It must be the suit, he could not think of any other reason for all of this, but that would be madness to assume, it would be pure insanity to think an inanimate suit was responsible for all of this torture.

How else can I explain this?

Suddenly he wished he had never applied for that Christmas vacancy, he wished he had just walked on by and let it pass from his memory, but the desperation for a job and money got the better of him. Now it wanted him. That creature he only thought existed in films and grim tales of monsters. It was causing all this chaos, preparing his state of mind for a horrifying journey. At that moment a man who sang festively about giving his heart away on Christmas day replaced the jingle about sleigh bells.

On the television he saw not the original music video, but another. In this version the 80s singer stabbed himself in the chest and ripped out his own beating heart and offered it to Santa. On his knees the singer smiled and breathed heavily as blood dripped through his fingers. Santa took the heart and ate it in one agonising mouthful, he smacked his lips together in satisfaction and laughed in his signature '*Ho, Ho, Ho!*' manner. Then it happened, the unspeakable horror, the one that almost tipped Carson back over the edge of sanity, plunging him deep into the well of madness. The red and white figure on the television turned its head, moving like a wooden doll, the screen glitched and the static maggots briefly appeared, then Santa, that jolly old bastard from the Coke adverts smiled directly at him. It was not a jolly smile like you would imagine, it was a smile full of malice and with each glitch it transformed into something horrific, something you would only see in your darkest nightmares.

Tainted pale skin leaked onto Santa's face, like a thick layer of make-up, the teeth yellowed and became like chunks of discoloured ivory, and the eyes burned with ferocity and became something reptilian. It was an impish face and had long flowing dark hair with a single golden streak running through his fringe. Carson wanted to look, and he desperately wanted to look away, he wanted to see what this foul thing would look like, but he wanted to snatch his gaze away from that box and run outside in the snow. He wanted to make snow angels and die from hypothermia.

He wanted to die.

Anything but look that that horrible creature on the television, but curiosity killed the cat, and Santa would kill him too. The sinister Saint Nick sang his own creepy interpretation of the song on the television:

"Once bitten and always mine, you keep your distance, but I'll still eat you alive, tell me, Carson, do you recognize me? Well, I wouldn't worry, you'll soon get to know me. Merry Christmas, I wrapped you up inside me, with the notion that you'll never be free, I mean it. Now you know where it all begins, but if you kiss me now it will be your grisly end."

Santa's smile widened almost consuming his face. The festive monster laughed, it was a laugh that sounded like a thousand dying children and reached for him through the television, breaking the walls of reality. Carson screamed, he wailed for his sweet dear life and before his voice could become raw and before Santa could grab his face and peel his skin.

It stopped.

Normality was restored.

10

He ran into the kitchen, his thoughts spinning in berserk fashion as he grabbed a sharpened blade from the knife rack. It was a reckless attempt to end his life, but he was desperate and in that heated moment it seemed as if it were the only way. He touched the blade to his flesh, then drew back almost instantly. Something prevented him from carrying out that miserable deed, and he slammed the knife on the kitchen table in frustration. Carson breathed, then slumped on the cold vinyl floor and wept quietly so as not to disturb his dormant family.

The pavements were thick with sheets of snow, but the roads were not so bad thanks to the salt trucks that had made the rounds the night before. Getting into work was not as hard a chore as Carson had hoped. He wanted to take the day off, more so he wanted to quit completely, but that force which had stopped him from ending his life also ceased him from calling Tanya and telling her he could not carry on at Carmen's Curiosity

Emporium. He felt drawn to that place, like that suit was compelling his

every move.

 Those haunting glassy eyes stared at him, they stared through him and he

stared right back, almost like he was challenging whatever lurked

underneath its wickedly woven fibres. It was not his desire to dress up again,

he did not lust for the soft interior of that devilish suit, he wanted to run, he

wanted to burn it into ash and bury it deep beneath the frozen earth. But he

could not. Instead, the glassy eyes looked upon him with mind numbing

apathy, and he slipped inside the fabric for another day of spreading

Christmas cheer.

11

His skin tingled and began to itch, he scratched through the textile and his flesh felt abruptly hot, like he was lying on a scolding radiator. Carson grumbled with discomfort and heard maniacal laughter surround him, at every turn this malevolent noise spewed from every nook and cranny in the walls. He exhaled deep and counted to ten, yet the hallucinations did not subside. His skin grew more torrid and sweat poured out of his flesh, at least he thought it was sweat, it did not feel like sweat. It felt slimy, like mucus and as it painted his body, it tickled and caused him to itch intensely. Carson scratched like a barbaric beast and cried out in dismay. With desperate tugs he tried to pull off the suit, but it was fruitless, the Santa costume seemed to be fused to him. Now he screamed, but with every loud outburst the world around him seemed to fade, and he knew how one must feel when in the deathly coil of a constrictor snake. The walls peeled like rotting flesh, great chunks of plaster sagging to the floor with rubbery consistency. Pimples formed in wake of the wall and popped like fragile beads, they oozed a glutinous golden liquid that looked like honey mixed with soft cheese, and the smell was rank, like the interior of a bloated and decaying carcass. Carson clenched his jaw hoping it would snap, anything to take his mind off the agony surging through him. It started to feel as though someone had thrown acid over his body, that bitter melting sensation.

Let the bells ring out for Christmas!

Somewhere, far away, he could hear that song and it was maddening. The pain became unbearable and Carson's vertical state declined until he wound up on the floor of some unknown realm. In a frenzied attempt to be free from the bonds of that costume, he grabbed the fabric on his arm and yanked, it tore exhaled a sickening yelp of pain. The suit was alive!

As he stripped away the material, he felt nauseous at the sight of his skin peeling away from his arm. His eyes bulged in horror as he saw his flesh coming away from bone like slow cooked meat. Carson released his grip and the suit's fabric snapped back into place and healed itself.

"When the Krampus brings the fright, upon this Christmas night, he's put a child in his sack, with a fiendish smile on his face. If you jump into your bed I'll bite off your frightened head, even if you lock the doors, you can't escape the hungry Santa Claus"

227

The singing sounded like cockroaches skating on ice, it drove him into an insane rage. Now he slammed his fists upon a blackened wall hoping he could shatter the glass-like surface. Carson felt his skin melting inside the suit and in that moment he knew what was happening.

It's digesting me. Oh fuck! It's eating me and digesting me! Fuck! Help me!

But he could not talk. His lips had been disintegrated. He struggled to combat the deplorable suit. No, it was not a suit, it was a thing, a creature, and he had to remind himself it was no longer a case of battling an inanimate costume. But the more he fought, the faster it digested. It all came to a chilling conclusion when Carson seized the head mask in both hands, and before it could absorb those pieces of meat, he wrenched off the mask and the vile creature exuded a blood curdling squeal. Carson cried out in an agonising howl as the skin on his face was torn off in one ghastly, revolting pull. He threw the mask and it rolled along the ground, when it stopped it glared at him with those haunting glassy eyes. The raw naked muscles on his face pulsed and tormented him. A contorted and delirious laugh erupted like toxic volcanic ash from the holes within the Santa mask, the world was sent into a maddening spin and Carson felt dazed. He collapsed, passing out as he fell.

The mask quivered and the wax-like face metamorphosed into something ungodly, it sprouted slick tentacles and slithered towards the unconscious body of its victim.

It left a trail of coagulated grease in its wake and an odious smile appeared on its blasphemous face. The tentacles reached like elongated, mutated arms, they clung to Carson's head and the repulsive critter hauled itself back onto the corpse of its prey. It continued to assimilate Carson, breaking down every fabric of his being for sustenance, it was a nonchalant process that lasted 47 hours until nothing remained, not even bone.

Epilogue

There were worms wriggling in her stocking, they made an abominable sound, like someone kneading a bag of moist noodles. She dared not touch it, she did not want it to split open and spill whatever repugnant creatures lurked within. The record player emitted classic Yuletide music. The vinyl scratched and created a soothing background ambiance that was very appropriate for that kind of traditional music. Soon the pacifying quality slipped into something eerie, something she only expected to hear in her nightmares. There was a log fire in her home and it crackled. Before the hysteria had begun she was roasting chestnuts. Now, they had burned into charcoal rocks and popped, the noise spooked her. Some of the chestnuts hatched like eggs and birthed beetles that scuttled out of the flames and onto the marble fireplace. They crawled. It was a never-ending stream of insects. Laughter erupted and it was an all too familiar exclamation:

"Ho, ho, ho!"

Tanya Tatton shuddered.

It had been just under a year since she last thought of Carson Elwin, her former employee who disappeared on Christmas Eve. She went through the palaver of police interviews and late-night phone calls from his distraught parents for two weeks. She decided to move herself and the shop to another location, to somewhere faraway where she could forget about that poor guy and his broken family. This year she decided not to hire anyone to dress in the Santa suit, instead Tanya took on that role. Now she was beginning to understand, now it all started to make sense.

That confounded suit.

The television snapped on of its own accord, and static maggots clambered around the screen, the image adjusted and revealed an icy world where a turquoise aurora borealis ruled the skies like an enormous river. It was dazzling, but at the same time, extremely haunting. Then she saw him.

It.

Kris Kringle.

Not of flesh and blood though, but of that suit, that damned despicable suit. It waved to her and gnarled its wax-like face into something resembling a smile. Tanya wanted to scoop her eyes out with her fingers, she did not want to see it, she begged not to see it and fell to her knees to plead with it. In response it howled out genuine jolly laughter and clutched its rotund stomach in unison. Tanya screamed.

It spoke to her in a grizzled tone of voice:

"Twas the night before Christmas, when all around the house, vulgar creatures are stirring, even beneath your night blouse. You want your neck hung, by the chimney with care, but Kris Kringle is watching, so you will not dare. Instead, you'll be nestled all snug in your bed, with visions of us dancing inside your head. I will gobble you all up, with one vicious snap, and finally settle down for my long festive nap."

It reached for her through the television and its hands pierced the barrier between fantasy and reality. Tanya wanted to snatch herself away, but she was paralyzed with fear.

Oh God, I can't move!

She struggled to move but could not break free from the ghostly shackles that kept her bound to her living room floor. The hands were inches away from her face and stretched like ghoulish plasticine. Tanya wailed and the world around her seemed to collapse, and in its place she found herself in that icy world, the turquoise aurora palpitating above her. She closed her

eyes and wept. The beetles crawled over her body; she could feel them

scampering all over her flesh.

When she opened her eyes Tanya could see the hands in front of her face,

but before it could grab her face, before it could tear her skin asunder.

 It stopped.

Normality was restored.

The End

DEAD CHRISTMAS

Prologue

Blood dripped from the glistening scimitar. It was brooding crimson plasma and it congealed quickly. He gazed out in helpless horror at the familiar sights around him, which he perceived through eyes that were now alien. He was a prisoner within his own mind. The cold blade touched his lips and he felt his tongue lick the steel like it was an ice-lolly. The metallic taste of copper filled his mouth and he wanted to wince away from the fierce flavour, instead he saw his hijacked body lustily licking the scimitar clean. Mounds of corpses lay at his feet, the bodies of those he loved. Little people he had known for thousands of years, little people with big hearts, now dead by his hand. The world was catastrophic and from within his cage he cowered and cried and refused to accept there was an invading force inside him. His right hand shot out with uncanny speed and grabbed someone attempting to flee. He held the little creature by his neck and squeezed.

'Why are you doing this Father?' said the elf. His eyes widened in terror and slowly they began to protrude like ripening fruit. With his left-hand Father snatched those gelatinous globes out of the elf's skull and stuffed them greedily into his mouth. When he bit down they popped like fattened beetles, and tendrils of blood and vitreous dribbled out of his mouth. The elf released an excruciating howl. He felt his lips widen into a grin and something stirred in his baggy trousers, something that pulsed with ferocity. Something that swelled into an uncontrollable urge. The elf squirmed in his hand, such a tiny and delicate little thing he was wailing and writhing and trying to break free even though his fate was sealed. The big man, that once loving and proud man, pulled down his trousers and freed that throbbing uncontrollable urge. A whimpering kind of silence fell upon them. The elf ceased his struggles and came to terms with his death. Elves did not die of natural causes and rarely died otherwise, so this experience was extraordinary and he was curious to discover what lay beyond the crimson curtain of this world. The big man disapproved of this moment of clarity. In an act of wretched spite he pushed his quivering cock into the elf's gory moistened eye socket. The little creature leapt into a fresh frenzy and started his flesh-crawling shrieks once more. He did not want to watch his body defile the poor elf. He did not want to feel the hideous cocktail of pleasure and humiliation stroking his sensitive area. All he could do was watch

236

because he had no other option. Whatever had hijacked his body wanted him to watch and it wanted him to suffer in the most abominable way.

The elf died haemorrhaging from various ruptured orifices, his body was cast away like a sack that had been emptied of its goods. The big man stalked through the field of cadavers searching for his next victim. His black boots clomped heavily and seemed to make the world shake around him. To his right he heard a noise, something he was very intimate with.

Jingle bells.

It was the first natural thought the hijacker had made since entering this body. The sound came from behind a pantry door made from a thick glossy wood. The handle was made of brass and it looked like a hefty door to open. The big man had no issues. The inside of the pantry exposed a frightened group of elves all huddled as if it would somehow protect them. One elf clutched a hat that had a cluster of golden bells on its tip.

'Jingle all the way,' he said and smiled.

Santa Claus smiled.

Chapter I

Night Starr usually experienced pleasant dreams full of festive delights during the countdown to Christmas. The ones he experienced on the twenty-third night of December were multifaceted nightmares containing themes that could only be described as abhorrent. Dreams of the Grotto falling to a nefarious force, masses of mutilated elves lay scattered upon the workshop floor, and at its nexus there was Santa. A once rotund man full of joy and festive fever was now a scrawny and feeble old man, with eyes full of tears and a mouth full of words spoken cryptically:

Night, my body has been compromised. She has returned. You must go deep into the Yule Tree Forest and diminish her hold over me. Beware.

The scene confounded him as the Christmas toys came to life and started munching on the walls of reality. They devoured the dream from the inside and exposed the void between the phantasmagorical world and the waking world. He knew it was an illusion. The lack of natural odours rendered the dream fraudulent, thus diminishing his fears. But there were the screams. They were tangible audible waves broadcasting through his brain, not his ears. Usually dream sounds were like noises made in an echo chamber that rippled through the distance of that fake reality. The screams brought back the fear and they only increased in volume. There was an odour, the faint aroma of charcoal enveloped his nose and in that moment of panic snapped him awake.

The Grotto was aflame.

Grotto was an affectionate term they all used. It was in fact a palace, gigantic and carved out of a vast cliff face. Great sheets of ice both transparent and frosted were used as roofs and windows. At night the walls reflected the starlight and moonlight, making it sparkle like fresh blankets of snow. It was an ancient structure forged by the first age of elves in the days when Santa was young and another Father Christmas reigned supreme. It had stood for thousands of years unharmed by nature and undiscovered by mankind, yet there it was a blazing inferno. Something had discovered it. Night Starr collapsed out of his cosy log cabin into the snow. He saw elves flooding out of the gates in mass exodus, creatures full of petrified sorrow.

From within the walls there erupted bellowing laughter. Not of the jolly

kind, it was the kind of laughter that brimmed with insanity and

enmity. The heat was so intense that Night failed to see his breath in the

cold winter air. Not all the elves attempted to flee. Some were busy trying to

douse the flames. Luckily it seemed like a contained fire and had not spread

to Santa's workshop or the reindeer shelter that was situated on the opposite

far side of the Grotto. Night was thankful.

 A sudden urge fell upon him to seek out Santa, and find out what kind

mischief had befallen the Grotto. He started for the gates but

 (Beware)

stopped after seeing a snippet of his dream. He grabbed a passing elf. She

let out a cry of terror then calmed as she saw who it was.

 'Night, thank the seasons you're all right. You should leave now. He's

coming for us all and it's useless to reason. He's gone mad,' she said as she

gasped for breath in the mixed temperature of the night.

 'What has happened Gloria? What is this chaos?' he asked laying his hands

on her shoulders. He caressed her and calmed the anxious little elf.

'It's Father Claus. Something has infested his mind and driven him to slay us all. I can't begin to describe the horrors I have seen, dear Night. Such things are for the human realm, not for us where the merriments of Christmas are our way of life. I'm afraid Christmas is dead, Night. I'm afraid there will be no more peace and goodwill for all mankind this December twenty-fifth. I'm afraid...'

She fell into his arms and wept. Night removed her elf hat and stroked her silver hair.

'Where will you go?' he said.

'Those of us who have survived are going into the Yule Tree Forest to seek out a path to the nearest village, or perhaps step through a Membrane into another world and leave this place forever.'

Another scene from his dream flickered before his eyes.

Diminish her hold over me.

'I'm coming with you, Gloria, but I'm not running away from my home. I'll find a way to stop this. Christmas is not dead,' he said.

'Yet.' She replied and sniffled.

'Will you help me?'

'Night, I've seen things. We've all seen things that no elf has ever seen. You are yet to see those loathsome acts but you will. *Then* you will understand! Don't expect me to help you to the end. Even if you manage to save Christmas things will never be the same. We will never be the same.'

'So be it.'

He took her hand and his warmth made her smile momentarily. They trudged through the snow into the Yule Tree Forest. Behind them those bellowing cries of laughter exploded again.

Chapter II

The Yule Tree Forest was a colossal gathering of fir trees that stretched for miles across the land. If you were to navigate your way through that dense forest, you would find yourself at the foot of a mountain range that served as the border for North Pole. The trees themselves reached hundreds of feet into the heavens. They were all wrapped in sheets of snow and despite their density the snow always made its way to the forest floor. It was a magical and mystical place that remained mostly unexplored. Those who endeavoured to journey beyond the surveyed lands seldom returned to speak of their encounters.

 Night, Gloria, and the elves that fled to seek refuge were unaware of how far the forest's magical tapestry extended, since they had all led mostly sheltered lives in Santa's Grotto. It was an alien experience for them all. Night ventured into the unknown. He was not prepared for undertaking such a task as saving Christmas. For now, he followed Gloria northward, using her compass to guide them. He knew the answer was out there somewhere and it would reveal itself in due time. They looked all around at the snow-coated foliage and the gigantic trees above them. Gloria noticed strange spherical shapes dangling from the branches.

'They look like baubles, but who would decorate a place so big?' she said.

'They are natural fruiting bodies. They grow every December and each individual fruit has its own unique intricate pattern traced upon its skin. Father told me they inspired him to popularise the tradition of hanging baubles on Christmas trees,' said Night.

'You were his elf advisor, Night. Didn't you notice anything strange about him?'

He cast his thoughts upon the previous night and remembered nothing suspicious about Santa, although...

'The aurora had a queer look to it. The lights in the sky took on a sickly amaranth glow. I asked Father if it's anything we should be concerned about. He seemed distracted. I thought nothing of it considering how close we were to the big day, you know he he's been more and more off in recent years. I think the stress of modern life and demands of modern children are finally weighing him down. I didn't think it would turn him to murderous rage.'

Gloria looked away and focused her attention once more on the trees. Her mind was awash with ghastly memories of a past that was too recent to bury.

'This place is peaceful,' she said.

'Yes it is, but I do not trust it. Don't ask me why.'

'Why?'

Night noticed a mischievous smile cover her face as she asked. Santa's elves were renowned for their simple and childish humour and even during this sinister time it warmed his heart to see her keeping to one of their core values: humour builds a happy home, as his elf-mother used to say.

He wondered how long it would last.

Dawn steadily approached from the east. As the snow poured through the trees like clouds of ash the light was somehow stifled. The forest was murky and Night longed to see the shards of daylight piercing the gloom – but it did not come to pass. Instead, the world around him seemed ominous, like the umbrage was clawing back secrets and hiding them within its dark heart. It had been hours since they entered the Yule Tree Forest, and still they had not encountered any form of life, elf or otherwise. They were about to settle down for some respite when Gloria spied an ice cabin up ahead. Smoke

plumed from its transparent chimney.

'Maybe they can help,' she said.

Night was desperate for any form of aid in the sudden quest, which had

been bestowed upon him from his dream-father. They decided to approach.

After all, they had no choice.

Chapter III

North Pole elves were immune to the deathly bite of cold. It had been hard wired into their genetics since the ancient times, before Santa Claus emancipated them from slavery. This made their trek through the forest far less arduous. Night and Gloria were experiencing temperatures that would kill a mortal creature within moments.

As they lumbered towards the ice cabin Gloria noticed the faint sound of jingling bells. She looked around and was unable to trace the sound upon the current of the wind. Night seemed to be paying no mind to this pleasant music that had suddenly materialised from nowhere. Then she noticed a small leather pouch hanging from his belt. It seemed to be the source of the sound.

'What's in the pouch, Night? That music is beautiful,' she said.

He looked down at the swinging little sack nonchalantly and replied:

'This old thing? This is a pouch of magic powder. To be more precise it contains the ashes of a once powerful deity. This is what makes the reindeers fly on Christmas Eve. Father entrusts it to me and I guard it and apply it to those majestic beasts when the time comes.'

'What's with the jingle bells?'

'No one knows. Father once told me it's the sound of festive adoration, though I think he was just being poetic. This stuff is the reason why jingle bells exist as a Christmas tradition. When the reindeer are covered in it the sound is stronger, and it flows with their movements as they glide through the Christmas sky. The reason why you can hear them now is because the big day approaches and the ashes are excited.'

'Doesn't it ever run out?'

'The ashes of a God never wither away.' Night caught the eye of his companion and smiled. 'I know you're a new elf Gloria so don't be afraid to ask questions.'

She blushed in the winter air. Her cheeks flushed with rouge splotches that were emphasised by the startling white world around them.

'I'm sorry, Night. I was only created this summer solstice. I still have a lot to learn.'

'That's quite all right. There is a lot to learn but the best thing about it is you have an eternity to familiarise yourself with the Grotto and all its rich history.'

Gloria smiled. Her eyes coruscated despite the lack of light amongst the trees. It made them appear more like rare jewels to be marvelled at in a world full of rocks. There was still a hint of melancholy on her face.

'This was to be my first Christmas. I have been preparing since my creation for the festive season to come, and now it's dead.'

Night went to give her an encouraging yet affectionate touch on the shoulder when something collided with her head and sent her sprawling across the snow. It was a globe of ice. Blood steadily seeped into the snow and spread like ink on tissue. Before Night could tend to her wound a globe of ice struck him too.

The world darkened and with it came dark figures that cackled and waddled, scooping them up before carrying them into the unknown.

Chapter IV

He experienced another of those dreams. It was vivid yet lacked certain qualities associated with either the waking world or the dream world. He was no longer in the forest and found himself in a cosy room with a roaring log fire and a burgundy leather chair opposite. By the chair was a small table with an unfinished glass of sherry on its surface. Surrounding him were vast quantities of books divided into various genres ranging from fictional to historical to poetical and even hermetical.

I'm in Father's lodge.

He felt no warmth emitting from that blazing furnace, neither did he feel the cold of the forest. The literature lacked substance, and the sherry appeared dull.

You're in my subconscious, a voice spoke from behind one of the shelves. *What's left of it anyway.*

Father, is that you? Show yourself, I beg.

From behind a bookcase that housed a wealth of knowledge about the mind, there appeared that same malnourished man he encountered in his previous dream. Scraggy Santa was how Night came to think of him, though it pained him to do so.

We haven't much time, Night. She is searching for me. She wants to eradicate whatever morsel of myself exists in this invaded body. This is my sanctuary, but I fear not for long.

Who is she Father? What has happened to you?"

I've been consumed by an ancient evil. Perahta. That is her name.

But who is she? Father what is...

The air was suddenly filled with malice. It was a sensation that was neither cold nor hot. It was a state of mind that could not be comprehended on any conscious level. It was something only experienced deep in the bowels of the darker self, those corners we wish never to visit.

She is close. Night, listen to me. East from where you are now there is a cave. It is the only cave in the forest and inside is a man, a hermit of sorts. He is a great sage. You must gain his help, for only he can stop this damnable force. He is the one who cast her out before.

How will I know who to find?

Scraggy Santa laughed and it was as flaccid as his figure, yet Night was filled with hope. Maybe there was still time.

I think you'll recognise him. Use the ashes to fly back to the Grotto. I warn you though you must not use it to get there! As she consumes my power the magic within that dust will fade, using it more than once will deplete it rapidly.

Night reached out hoping to touch his mentor, his friend, his father. Instead, the vision melted like wax.

You're in grave danger, Night. You must wake up and run. The forest is no longer safe. Her nefarious hands have touched it and made it rotten. Wake up."

Chapter V

The need for urgency engulfed his mind. His body jolted and his eyes flickered open. The figures standing around him made him yelp with fright. Surrounding him were four snowmen. Their charcoal eyes stared down at him, full of inky indifference. Their faces were contorted as if they were trying to sneer. Night shivered as dread influenced his thoughts. He lay on a slab of thick ice, and though he could feel the cold temperature it did not inconvenience him. He was also aware of being inside the ice cabin that he and Gloria had spied earlier on. The sinister snowmen continued to gaze down on him like beings from another world. Before he could articulate himself and ask where they had taken Gloria, they started to waddle away. Their movements appeared clumsy at first, but then he noticed the polished ice helped them to glide across the floor. The room Night found himself in was festive and tinsel traced the room with sparkling delight. Faux snowflakes dangled from the ceiling in droves and on the walls were wreathes of holly. At the foot of the bed, for that is what he lay on, there was a Nutcracker doll dressed in the garments of a king. That too stared at him with inky indifference, though he doubted this object was a live creature.

You're different.

Night found it difficult to deduce whether he heard the voice in his mind, or if it had actually been spoken.

'Who said that?'

He felt stupid asking that question. After all he already knew the answer. It was staring right at him.

You're different.

He assumed the voice was in his head, as the Nutcracker's mouth did not open.

'Are you with them?'

No need to beat around the holly bush.

No, I'm just as much a victim as you. The only difference is that they want to keep me alive so I can watch. Did I mention you're different?

'Yes, you did. How am I different?'

They haven't disembowelled you yet. The others are dangling from hooks shedding their blood and entrails onto the icy floor. They have kept you alive for some reason. Are you important?

'That's not an answer I know, as I'm not familiar with these things. Do you know where Gloria is? She was with me when they captured me.'

Her body is safe, for now. But her mind is in peril. Would you fancy getting out of here?

'That's an answer I do know: yes!'

Splendid! We shall save your companion then get out of here.

A strange sensation penetrated Night's eyes. The Nutcracker King shimmered the way objects would shimmer in rising heat. A mirage in the room, gone for a brief moment before reappearing by the room's frosty door.

'Can't you just perform that trick to escape?'

There is a magical veil shrouding this cabin. I can only move within it.

Then came the screams that made Night's flesh crawl, and bumps formed on his skin like scabies and hysteria clawed at his heart.

'Gloria! No!'

He rushed to the door, being careful not to slip on the ice and peered into the next room. What he saw nearly caused him to vomit. The Nutcracker King was right, from the ceiling dangled the cadavers of elves. Their flesh had been torn asunder and their organs lay upon the floor and had been arranged into various festive shapes. Their bodies had been carved and shaped into snowflakes and some beast had made snow angels in the pools of blood. Night wanted to cry. He didn't witness the horror at the Grotto. He imagined it would have looked like this.

The forest is no longer safe. Her nefarious hands have touched it and made it rotten.

That's what Santa had said in his vision.

'She knows I'm here and she knows what I am trying to do,' he said.

Who is she?

'Her name is Perahta, as for what she is I...'

Perahta! No, it cannot be! My friend we need to abdicate this prison at once. Suddenly it has all been made very clear.

Night understood the desperation of the situation and therefore did not press on with more questions. He pulled open the cold hunk of door and stepped out into the gruesomely festive abattoir.

The blood had not coagulated on the ice. The puddles were still hazardously moist and Night had to manoeuvre delicately if he wanted to avoid detection. On the opposite side of the room he spied an elf still alive, trussed up and hanging from the ceiling like his dead brothers and sisters. Night recognised him.

'Norman...'

Be quiet, said the Nutcracker King. *They are coming.*

They hid behind a large oak desk that housed the various implements used to torture and mutilate the elves. From another room appeared a snowman. Its expressionless face scanned the abattoir then it turned its attention upon Norman. The little creature pleaded for his life and begged it not to harm him. He even offered his eternal service in exchange for his life. His cries for mercy fell upon deaf ears. The sadistic snowman brandished a sharpened axe and waved it in front of Norman's face, tormenting him. If it took pleasure in watching the elf suffer, it showed no signs of declaration. Night squirmed

behind the desk. He wanted to leap out and save his comrade, but knew it

would result in his own death.

I think your friend is in that other room, along with the rest of the

snowmen. They must be eradicated.

'How can I? Look at what they're capable of,' whispered Night.

Before the Nutcracker King could reply there was a sickening secretion of

sound, like a watermelon smashing against a wall. The axe connected with

Norman's head dead centre. Blood puked from the wound in ghastly squirts

and his body twitched in his bonds. The snowman nodded its rotund head.

Its dazzling white body was spattered with tinges of crimson blots.

Night, it's now or never.

'How do we stop them?'

Fire.

The Nutcracker King had a trick of his own. When he moved in that

bewildering and shimmering way, he was actually flitting between

dimensions. He wanted to be free, and he wanted to aid Night on his quest

to save Christmas and rid the world of Perahta. He knew that it could possibly mean his own death, but that didn't matter for he knew that it would not be in vain. He had wanted to do this for a while and held off in fear of wasting his life. Night saw the Nutcracker King glisten and ripple like water after it's disturbed by a rock. Mere seconds passed by and then with spasmodic ferocity he returned immersed in dazzling flames that he had captured from some fiery dimension.

Find Gloria, save Christmas, and remember me.

Night was astounded by this astonishing display of heroics. The Nutcracker King no longer shimmered. It ran towards the snowman and moved like a normal bipedal creature, except with extraordinary speed. Soon the ice cabin was ablaze and melting.

Night found Gloria unconscious in a room full of shrieking and dissolving snowmen. The sounds exuding from them were like cracking ice and howling wolves. It set Night's teeth on edge. He stopped in his tracks and saw the flaming Nutcracker King shimmering in and out of reality, bringing with him more fire and sending the cabin into a treacherous inferno. He scooped Gloria into his arms and carried her outside into the forest. As the ice cabin liquefied the flames were doused and all that remained were smouldering ashes from the surrounding woodland that churned thick plumes of smoke. Nothing remained of the Nutcracker King. Whether he had perished or fled to another world, Night would never know. Nothing remained of anything. Night sneezed repeatedly as his senses had been irritated by the aftermath. Once the fits had subsided, he focused his attention on pulling Gloria from whatever barren dreamscape those damned snowmen had sent her to. When he touched his hand to her brow, he was overwhelmed with images of freakish creatures that were transitioning between human and reindeer. They were dead creatures and their feculent bodies were contorted in ways that made them look like abyssal sea monsters washed up on the black sands of Iceland. He snatched away his hand and fought back tears of revulsion. What kind of nightmarish land had they sent her to?

Those deplorable brutes.

He carried her through the forest. As the hours slipped away so did his hope of her returning to him. He felt isolated and the sounds of supernatural

activity in the forest made him nervous. Not even the sound of the jingle
bells could soothe him.

Gloria awoke abruptly and her immediate grip on his shoulders almost
startled him to the ground. Her eyes were as glacial as the forest and in them
he saw a face, distorted and ghastly.

'I have seen her, Night. I have seen Perahta. She's coming for you. Our
time grows short. The forest is evil,' she said as her eyes flickered in and out
of consciousness.

'Stay awake Gloria, wherever you are being called back to, don't go. There
is nothing for you there but misery. You don't want to be a child of misery,'
said Night.

Her eyelids managed to stay open. Those jelly-like gems still did not
recognise him, and his sorrow nearly tossed him over the edge into insanity.
There was an instant in which he wanted to violently shake her from her
coma. Before the insanity could fully manifest, her eyes locked on to his and
the acknowledgment in her eyes managed to console his grief.

She smiled and he kissed her brow.

They sat in front of a campfire that evening, the fire offering them protection against whatever dwelled amongst the firs.

'What happened when you saw her?' said Night.

'I was being chased through a cave by rabid robins. Their beaks frothed and their red breasts glowed with bloody intensity and guiding them was her. Perahta. I didn't see her in physical form, but when I turned I could have sworn the robins formed the shape of a misshapen face. In my head I heard a nursery rhyme, except the words were different. She sang to me. It was a lullaby of death.'

Gloria shuddered and sang a rhyme that curdled Night's blood and for a moment he really felt the cold.

No Christmas for your children,

I'll snatch them from their bed,

You'll find them dead tomorrow,

And be driven out of your head.

Their stomachs will be cut open,

Stuffed with coal and dead light,

You'll scream on Christmas morning,

And weep through Christmas night.

No fireplace, no Santa,

No more festive cheer with friends,

Only my fire and wicked fury,

As Christmas slowly ends.

For me I have no pity,

Your sorrow stronger proves,

Because your naughty children

Have been buried along with you.

Something yelped in the distance. They stared into the strange aura of the night and huddled closer together.

'She kept singing it as those robins chirped with bloodthirsty joy. They would have torn my veins out of my flesh. I know it. They wouldn't have stopped until I was nothing but a little skeleton,' she said and broke into tears. 'Then I heard you calling me and I realised I wasn't supposed to be in that cave. I wasn't supposed to be a child of misery.'

She held him tight.

'Do you know what those snowmen were doing to you in that room?' said Night.

Gloria shook her head. It was enough for him and he could tell she did not want to speak of it again. The jingle bells were growing louder. The dawn of Christmas Eve approached and their time waned.

Chapter VI

Morning crept across the sky like an octopus stretching its tentacles across the ocean floor. The fir trees allowed streaks of light to penetrate their branches and scatter throughout the forest. Night woke Gloria from her slumber. She roused with ease, signifying she had not been dreaming.

'Didn't you sleep?' she asked while wiping her eyes.

'No. I could not face Father again. The last time he appeared to me he looked gaunt, a shadow of the man he once was. I am too afraid to see how he looks now.' He said this with a hint of woe, which he tried to hide. Gloria noticed it and she kissed his cheek.

The immaculately frozen forest was ruptured by a terrible blizzard, a swirling wall of snow impeding their vision. Night had no doubt it was Perahta who controlled the hindering storm. They challenged this disturbance, not allowing it to prevent them from reaching their goal, but the harder they fought, the harder the blizzard raged. Night thought he saw shadowy figures moving amidst the thick swirling snow. No creature would surely dare to brave this weather, not unless it had a purpose like he and Gloria. The sounds of jingling bells had been replaced by the ululating cyclone and they could not find their way through the forest. With each passing arduous step their hope declined and on one occasion Gloria fell to her knees exclaiming she could not move any further.

'Leave me to die here, it's useless. Perahta is too powerful. Christmas is dead,' she said, breaking down into tears. Night plucked her onto her feet, and with a loving tenderness began to brush the snow from her colourful clothes.

'We are not dead, so neither is Christmas,' he said.

The shadowy figures stirred again and this time they seemed closer. Night wiped his eyes. His vision had become impaired by the flurries of snow.

'What's wrong?' said Gloria.

'I don't know. I thought I saw something.'

All at once his fears were proven correct. Out of the blizzard came erratic humanoids. Their skin was pale, their eyes like polished ivory stones, and their naked bodies hairless. From their backs protruded great wings with dirty white feathers. They shrieked like the storm and reached out for Night and Gloria, the pair using their small size to dodge the tall slender creatures. The rabid insanity these beings possessed pushed against Night's sanity. He had seen things elves were not meant to see. His species was an innocent one, deprived of depraved images involving violence and daemons. The humanoids had long unkempt nails that had twisted into strange tentacle claws, and with these they tried to tear the elves' flesh. The things disappeared back into the storm then reappeared with such suddenness it almost bewildered the two elves into submission. Night struggled to keep count of how many of the things there were. For all he knew it was only two, and they were using the blizzard to their advantage.

 Then there was nothing. For a while the attacking ceased and Night thought the things had given up. He clutched Gloria hoping his mind did not unravel. He was struggling to keep hold of his faculties. His body quivered and he summoned all of his will to settle. Then Gloria spoke with terror:

 'Oh no. Night. Oh no! No!'

Out of the snowy gloom appeared seven of those winged humanoids. They advanced in slow movements and encircled the two elves. Their postures brought a moment of clarity to Night.

'They're angels. Gloria, they're angels!'

'Then why do they intend to harm us?'

He could not answer. His sanity slipped and he started to laugh. It was all he could do. Perahta would win. She had found him. Lavish bursts of merriment exploded from his mouth. Gloria pushed herself away from him and her face was a picture of shock and horror. Night roared with laughter as the angels made their move.

Something else came out of the storm and it too was laughing:

'Ho! Ho! Ho!'

Chapter VII

A large man clad in green and white robes stepped out of the storm. He was a tremendous figure of a man both large in height and width and he bellowed with festive cheer. The angels turned their attention on him, and upon doing so their faces contorted into something wicked and absurd. The large man raised his arms in a welcoming gesture and what followed brought Night and Gloria close together in a protective huddle. The angels quivered, their bodies trembling with frightening speed, and one by one they popped like gelatinous pimples. Their supernatural flesh disintegrated into webs of blood and bone and a creamy viscous fluid that could not be described by any mortal being. The two elves were smothered with the strange residue of those beings and their confusion transformed into fright as they expected to be next. Instead, the large man stepped through the snowy haze and with a confident flick of his robes dispelled the blizzard.

'Don't be afraid my children. I am a better man than those you have encountered along the path, come and know me,' said the large man who looked at them with a comforting smile. Night was taken back by the familiarity of that face.

'Santa?' he asked in astonishment. The large man bellowed festively again.

'Not quite, my child, I am his predecessor Saint Noel, though Noel will do just fine. What brings you out here my little elves?'

'I know now who we have been looking for. It is you, Noel. Santa is in trouble and he needs help and you seem to be our only hope.'

A mixed look of curiosity and concern washed over Saint Noel's face.

'What seems to be ailing Santa these days? He's still a young soul from what I recall,' he said.

'He has been taken by one known as Perahta,' said Gloria. Noel's face lit up in agony and he grabbed the two elves and lifted them up and carried them way with him.

'My apologies but we don't have time, we must go,' he said.

They were taken to a cave. A boulder obstructed the entrance. On it the words *Noel's Hollow* were chiselled into the rock, and painted green and white. Noel pushed the stupendous spherical stone aside with great ease, as if it were made of polystyrene. The interior of the hollow had no trace of commercial festivity in its decorations; the halls were decked with more traditional adornments. Dried oranges and lemons hung from the lush moss covered, walls, along with sticks of cinnamon, and gingerbread shaped like all things associated with Christmas.. The aromas were exquisite and made the elves' mouths salivate with hunger. Wild holly grew in natural wreaths, and plump shiny berries clung in between the leaves. It inspired awe in Night. His eyes were feasting and savouring the sights around him. He had always thought that hollows were cold and dirty earthy places. This one was warm and snug and smelled of all the things that made him happy. Then he remembered what his Father had said to him, that the forest was rotten, and his suspicion grew.

'Welcome to my humble abode dear elves. I wish I could say make yourselves at home, but we no longer have time for hospitality,' said Noel.

'It's remarkable,' said Gloria. Tears welled in her eyes.

'Yes it is. But how do we know you're not some cruel glamour created by Perahta?' asked Night.

'Said the king to the little elves, listen to what I say, pray for peace and trust in me, in my palace with a voice as big as the sea,' said Noel. A strange golden aura pulsated around him. It was welcoming, a sign of his honesty. The bag of magic dust sang choruses of jingle bells. Night smiled.

'You glow with the true light of Christmas my friend. Forgive me my doubts,' he said.

'Tis the season for forgiveness and love. Your doubts were not unfounded. Now we must go to task,' said Noel.

He led them to the centre of the hollow where there stood a humongous tree. It stood tall and thick, its branches splayed all across the ceiling, and in between them were sparkling stalactites of crystal. The tree itself had been hollowed out at the base. The entrance was eight feet tall and around the doorway Night saw tiny candy canes. Saint Noel stopped and Gloria and Night stopped with him.

'It is in here where I banished Perahta in the long-ago years. She was the anti-Santa, the one who punished all the bad children. Her role was to fill their dreams with grotesque images on Christmas Eve. The children would dream that their bellies were slit open and stuffed full of coal, and their stockings stuffed with their entrails. The idea was that they would wake up and turn their behaviour around and they would be good. It worked to some degree, for a long time, until Perahta was driven insane by the naughtiness in the world. She felt that it wasn't enough, that children wouldn't learn through fabrications alone. So one dark Christmas Eve she practiced her foul deeds for real. Many children died that night. I managed to stop her before the light of Christmas Day broached the sky. I captured her and brought her here to the hollow and banished her to the void for all eternity. I removed her essence from her physical form so she could not escape. But she must have made some dark pact with some cruel daemon in the space between worlds, for now she has returned and chosen your Santa to be her physical form. If she consumes his consciousness all will be lost. I curse myself for not seeing it sooner.'

Night placed a comforting hand on Noel's calf. It was the only place on the giant man's body he could reach.

'Santa is still in there. We still have time,' said Night.

Noel looked down at the two elves and his face beamed in a jolly smile that settled their frantic hearts.

'Then follow me into the tree where it all started and where it will end again,' he said.

Chapter VIII

Inside the tree there was a vast cavern. It was dark and moist and strange

vegetation grew on the walls unlike anything Night had ever seen. He heard

water dripping into pools and the sounds echoed into eternity.

'Did we step through a Membrane?' asked Gloria.

'We did, child,' said Noel. 'It is one of many that are scattered throughout

this forest. I guard this one because it contains a doorway into the void. After

I banished Perahta I decided to crown Santa as the new King of Christmas,

and remained here to make sure nothing would escape that wretched in-

between world. It seems all those years proved futile.'

As they advanced through the cavern Night and Gloria saw tiny creatures

emerging from cracks in the walls. They held tiny orbs of light in their hands

and they flew on rapidly beating wings.

'Night, look! Fairies! I never thought I'd ever see one,' said Gloria. Her

face was full of awe.

The fairies lit up the cavern, and what was revealed was an old workshop

with shelves full of vials. Some were empty and dusty but some contained fluids that represented the different colours of Christmas. There was an oak table that, to the elves, looked gargantuan and on it were various clay pots and pipettes and experimental tools designed for harnessing magic.

'This is where I come to perform parapsychological procedures. I have long been fascinated by the magic that inhabits the Yule Tree Forest and wish to learn its ancient secrets. Tonight, however, it will be a place where evil is summoned and hopefully cast out.'

'What do you plan to do?' asked Night. His attention was focused on the various vials stocked on the shelves.

'My plan involves what you're looking at now, my dear elf. By using the nativity potions I will summon Perahta in whatever ethereal form she manifests in, then cast her back into the void via that doorway there,' said Noel. He pointed towards a door at the far end of his workshop. It was a black door made of charcoal and upon the burned wood there were effigies of terrible tentacled monsters. Night thought it was very cliché but supposed any door that led into the void would look ominously malicious.

A distant noise bellowed through the tree's entrance. It was a trumpet.

'Oh no,' said Night. 'It can't be!'

'What is it?' said Gloria. She looked frightened and Night remembered it was her first Christmas. All of it was alien to her. It was one thing to learn about the trumpets, but another to actually hear them.

'The Christmas Trumpets, they signal the coming of Christmas Day. The first trumpet announces Santa's departure from the Grotto. The second announces when he's halfway around the world. The third announces his return to the Grotto. We're running out of time, we must hurry, Noel,' said Night.

The former Father Christmas grabbed two vials from the one of the shelves. A green one and a red one. He mixed them together and they produced a golden liquid that sparkled like the stars in heaven. Saint Noel drank the potion and began an incantation to summon the daemon:

Hark the herald angels sing,
'Return to us the Christmas King
His joy is eternal, his mercy mild
I want this Christmas reconciled.'
Perahta your evil will not rise,

Now return to me from among the skies,

With Yuletide authority I proclaim,

'Your actions are full of deceit and shame!'

Hark the herald angels sing,

'Return to us the Christmas King!'

The charcoal door swung open so hard Night was surprised that it didn't shatter into smithereens. The opening was so black it looked as though someone had mopped the wall in matte paint. From inside a great gust of wind was belched out of that hole and Saint Noel's body was sent into sickening spasms. Gloria held onto Night and the two looked on with helpless fright. Noel's spine suddenly arched and with it came a grotesque crack. He cried out in agony.

'Run my little elves! You must run!' he shouted through gritted teeth. His jaw clenched tight from the pain. The elves did not run. They could only watch in horror. Something had come through that door and Night knew what it was.

The flesh on Noel's back began to tear along his spine and blood splattered everywhere as a hand broke out from inside his body. The former Father Christmas let out one final gargling cry and blood spurted from his mouth and his body went limp. The hand that distended from his spine became two hands that tore his body in half, and beneath that discarded mutilated flesh was Perhata, in all of her physical gory glory covered in Noel's organs. She plucked those warm and gelatinous pieces of meat from her body and smiled wickedly at the two elves. Her mouth was wide and her dreadful smile showed multiple rows of teeth. Some were like sharpened sticks and others were like square blocks of ivory. Some for shredding and some for mashing and from her head protruded six ghastly crooked horns. There was an animal-like quality to her appearance. Not like any animal seen by any human, or elf. Gloria wondered if it had always been her physical form or if something had altered her in the void, twisted her and tore her apart and put her back together. Gloria could think about it no longer. Her mind shattered and she fell to her knees and screamed. Night fought hard to keep insanity at bay, but when that nauseating brown tongue flopped out of

Perahta's mouth and started licking her lips, he succumbed to madness and joined Gloria on his knees weeping and wailing.

Perahta laughed. The sound was like a dying donkey, and when she spoke the elves heard the sounds of all the children in the world crying.

'It is complete. The trumpets have announced my return! Now I will fulfil what I set out to achieve all those aeons ago, and you, my commiserable little abominations, can have two front row tickets to the death of Christmas and all the children in the world. Your precious Father is dead and those detestable beasts he rode upon are now meat for the maggots. Possessing his flesh was but a means to an end. I have you two to thank for my release.'

There was that laugh again, erupting like a volcano of noise, and a surge of adrenaline caused Night to shake off his breakdown. He grabbed Gloria and they ran for the forest.

'We have to go to the Grotto. We have to save Santa,' he said.

Gloria shivered in the cold. Their magic was fading as Christmas was dying.

'He's dead. There's nothing we can do but die with him,' she said.

'I cannot believe that! There has to be a way!'

But Scraggy Santa had stopped speaking to him. He had visions of that cosy part of Santa's subconscious now filled with snow and ice, where rabid snow rabbits gnawed at the walls and silver fish slowly devoured the books. It was a dead place and Scraggy Santa was nowhere to be seen.

The blizzard returned with ferocious force, and amidst the clouding snow Night saw the disfigured forms of the angels gathering and surrounding, preparing to tear them apart and send them to the void. Night unclipped the pouch of magical ashes. The jingle bells chimed and he felt Gloria's shivers calm in his arms. Her eyes were fixed on the sparkling dust Night produced from the pouch, the particles resembling a universe of stars twinkling in his hands. He sprinkled the ashes over himself and Gloria and they started to levitate off the ground. Gloria's grip tightened on his arm. Her eyes brimmed with sanity, a clarity that warmed the little elf's heart. They flew to the Grotto full of hope, leaving a glittery trail in their wake. If they could save Santa then they could save Christmas.

'We're flying!' she shouted over the blizzard. Her smile was enough to make Night fall in love.

Pillars of smoke bloomed over the horizon. The Grotto was a smouldering ruin devoid of its former festive glory. Their hearts sank at the sight, and as they entered, that sinking feeling descended further to the pits of their stomachs.

All around them lay the dead and dismembered and decaying corpses of their brothers and sisters. The place smelled of excrement and copper. Above the great golden staircase that led to Santa's quarters was the man himself, the former King of Christmas, crucified on a cross made of the bones of his beloved reindeer.

He died so that you two could live. Perahta's voice filled the air. *Now gaze upon my work and despair.*

The elves walked into the control room where there was a giant holographic screen, that used to enabled the other elves to live stream where Santa was in the world and watch the magic of Christmas unfold. Those elves were dead and their blood and vomit was strewn all over the control panels. The screen was fully functioning, only this time it showed the massacre of Christmas. Night and Gloria held each other close and watched helplessly as Perahta fulfilled her destiny.

The final trumpets called into the night and they lost their minds and despaired.

Epilogue

Mary woke up with a shiver. The morning was cold and an ivory frost had crystalised on the bedroom windows. It was nine o'clock and she was baffled at how long she had slept in, and the children too. Usually they were up and bouncing around the house like kangaroos on cocaine on Christmas morning. The night before had been a drain on them all. She had taken them to see extended family, including their crazy cousins who liked to play space exploration in the bedroom. This involved leaping off the bed onto the floor and walking around in slow motion pretending they were on some low-gravity planet, then there was the running around the house like they were traveling at warp speed, which was always cute and funny at first but soon became irritating. Mary never told them off for it, boys will be boys and besides it tired them out, which meant sleep would come quick for them. This didn't dispel her suspicions on Christmas morning though. No matter how quickly they fell asleep they always woke early to open their presents and probably fight over which one of them got the best ones. Then their dad would come round and take them to their grandmother's house for a couple of hours while Mary prepared and cooked the Christmas dinner. Every Christmas was like a set routine that never changed year by year. It never bothered her but Mary did wish her ex-husband had not had an affair and triggered the divorce. Then maybe they could have performed the Christmas ritual as a whole family. Never mind, Christmas wasn't a time for hindsight, not always, not now. It was a time for presents and food and lots of alcohol.

Maybe it's because the boys are getting older, and they've realised that the earlier they open their presents, the faster the excitement will be over.

But Joseph was eleven years old and Christian was thirteen. They were still at that age where they didn't consider the consequences of such things. It was Christmas and that meant presents at six in the morning.

Something doesn't feel right.

The foundations of her suspicions were strengthened when she entered each of the boy's rooms and found them empty.

'Joseph? Christian? Are you boys downstairs already? I hope you haven't opened your presents without me. Mummy will be very cross!'

Mary couldn't keep that concerned tone out of her voice. As she walked downstairs the floorboards beneath the carpet creaked. A sound that made her feel uneasy.

They probably waited downstairs for me then fell asleep on the sofa when I didn't wake up. That's it.

It had to be why she couldn't hear them making a fuss or bickering about which present to open first. Stepping off the stairs onto the hallway filled her with fresh trepidation. She couldn't shake off that stupid feeling of dread. It was ridiculous, why would something be wrong on a day like Christmas? She shook her body to loosen herself up and smiled.

'Right, let's wake these two up and begin the celebrations,' she said to herself.

Mary opened the living room door with confidence.

'Okay you two let's…'

First her knees gave way and she crumbled to the floor with no control, then she screamed with crystalline terror. The bodies of her two sons were propped up against the Christmas tree. Their bellies had been slit open and those gory wounds had been stuffed with coal and rotting oranges, dead robins and straw, and eerily pale glowing fairy lights. Their entrails were wrapped around the Christmas tree and the stockings that hung on the fireplace dripped with blood. It was later discovered they had been stuffed with the hearts and lungs of the two boys. Mary wretched and spewed bile over the linoleum floor of the living room. She couldn't bear going in. What kind of evil would do this to her family?

All over the world parents were waking up to find similar sights. Their children were dead, bellies cut open wide and filled with unsavoury things. All over the world Perahta's repugnant laugh echoed and all heard her poisonous proclamation:

No Christmas for your children,

I snatched them from their beds,

You've found them dead this morrow,

And are going out of your heads,

Their little fat bellies bled and bled

Upon my deathly sled,

Now you surely realise,

That Christmas is bloody dead!

THE GINGERBREAD
HOLOCAUST

Chapter One

Christmas morning dawned with sensational sunshine and settling snow. Kieran Gascoyne woke early with his sister and they sneaked downstairs. Kieran always opened his stocking first, it was a tradition he held dear for many years, and even at sixteen years old he still felt that nervous excitement in his stomach when discovering what wonders were stuffed into that woolly foot shaped sack. His mother and father usually packed their stockings full of traditional treats like candy canes, little Santa-shaped chocolates, mini jars of humbugs, green for him and purple for his sister, and a new snow globe to add to their Yuletide decorations. Every year their mother popped a special surprise in their stockings. His twelve-year-old sister found a Russian doll containing figures shaped like her favourite animals from the zoo. Kieran found a strangely decorated gingerbread man inside his stocking. One half of it had the motif of a traditional gingerbread man, and the other half was a skeleton with cartoon-like organs behind the bones. It was an odd surprise and he suspected it must have been his father's idea; the old man always had a flair for the macabre. The aroma that expelled from the biscuit made

Kieran's mouth water. On normal days he wouldn't dream of eating something so sweet before breakfast, but Christmas Day was no normal day, so he bit off the gingerbread man's head and chewed with delight. The ginger was not too overpowering and the icing was delicious. He contemplated saving some for later, but greed took over and he gobbled the whole thing down. His sister frowned at him.

"I wanted some of that," she said and folded her arms in a huff.

"Sorry," said Kieran, his mouth was full and he smiled at her, exposing half chewed biscuit. She grimaced and threw a slipper at him playfully.

When their parents finally roused from a peaceful slumber, they all began the long-held ritual of opening presents, saying their thanks, and exchanging hugs and kisses. Kieran came from a very wealthy family so their presents were always extravagant materials that the average citizen could not afford on a regular wage. Despite this, Kieran was a boy of simple pleasures and did not like to overindulge in extravagance. His sister, Barbara, looked up to him and he taught her to not be a spoiled brat and always be thankful for their fortunate position in life. So far, she had heeded his words wisely.

They lived in a stately home in countryside near the south coast of England. It had been passed down through the generations via their father's family line and was a tourist hotspot during the spring and summer seasons of the year.

Kieran's favourite thing about Christmas, apart from the quaint stocking fillers, was that his home was closed to the public for three weeks over Christmas and New Year. He hated not being able to enjoy the full comforts of home, so three weeks of peace and quiet were a welcome relief from the usual hustle and bustle. He would often ask his father if they could move to a place where they could enjoy their privacy and not have to share their home with complete strangers, but the old man was adamant about staying put and told Kieran that, as he grew older, he would come to understand family heritage was highly important. The boy didn't doubt his father, but still yearned for normality. But normality would never be a reality for him.

Chapter Two

The snow had fallen in great flurries overnight, and the home grounds were painted in a dazzling ivory white that sparkled in the sunlight like diamonds. At the centre of the garden was a gigantic pond, it was layered with a thin sheet of ice, and mother always warned her children not to go running on it lest they fall through and become frozen like those long lost, cavemen they saw in films. The topiary that gave the garden its title as a flamboyant spectacle was unrecognisable and looked like huge mounds of snow instead of elegantly shaped foliage. Kieran and his sister decided to take advantage of the white Christmas that had been bestowed upon them and after breakfast wrapped themselves up in warm clothing, including scarfs and gloves, and ventured outside into the Arctic Tundra, as Kieran liked to put it.

"Don't wander too far darlings, and don't stay out too long otherwise you'll catch your death," said Mother, kissing them both.

The first thing Barbara did when they ran outside was fall flat on her back and make snow angels. They both giggled and Kieran threw a snowball at his sister as she stood up.

"That's not fair!" she cried through laughter.

Thus began a snowball fight between brother and sister, their cheeks were rosy and ached from all the bellowing laughing. Once they ran out of breath they took some time to catch it again and decided to construct an epic snowman.

"It'll be the best snowman in all the south," said Kieran.

"You mean the world!" said Barbara.

Her brother smiled, but there was a hint of discomfort behind his eyes.

"Are you all right?" she said.

"Yes, my stomach just feels a bit sensitive. Maybe I shouldn't have eaten that gingerbread man before breakfast."

"You're silly. If you get too poorly maybe the snowman will come to life and be your servant for the day."

"I'll be fine Barb."

He kissed his sister on the head and they continued their fun but rather cold work.

Kieran's sensitive stomach quickly turned into turbulent storm of half-digested food. The cramps came with icky cruelty and he doubled over and dropped to his knees. His sister looked flabbergasted and covered her mouth with her hands.

"Oh my…" was all she could manage before her brother spewed out a great gush of brown putrid paste. It stained the purity of the snow.

"Mother! Father! Come quick! Something's wrong with Kieran!" Barbara shouted with all the volume she could summon.

The world quivered in his vision, Kieran heaved and more spoiled sludge ejected from his mouth. It looked like diarrhoea but smelled of sweet gingerbread biscuit. His body convulsed as if he were swimming in a sea of ice, but his temperature was burning like a furnace from hell. Before he passed out in the snow he muttered two words:

"Silly me."

Then fell flat on his face leaving behind a dead snow angel.

Chapter Three

He woke up on the sofa covered in a thin blanket in front of the roaring log fire, the cramps had subsided and the nausea was gone. His father was sitting on the reclining chair opposite.

"How are you feeling, Son?" he said while sipping a mug of hot chocolate.

"I feel better. How long have I been out for?"

"Only half an hour. What was that all about?"

"I think it was that gingerbread man you put in my stocking. I ate it before breakfast. Silly me."

His father frowned.

"I didn't put a gingerbread man in your stocking. Must have been your mother."

It was Kieran's turn to frown.

"How very odd," he said.

"Anyway, if you're feeling up to task you can come and help me lay the table while Barbara helps your mum prepare the Christmas dinner."

Father stood and left the room, taking a moment to ruffle his son's hair affectionately.

Kieran was overcome with a fierce itching sensation and when he threw back the blanket he noticed his arms were covered with dead skin, which he swore looked like biscuit crumbs. When he scratched his arms the flakes fell on the sofa like snow. He removed the t-shirt he was wearing and saw his whole torso was flaking. If his mother and father saw it they would cause too much of a fuss, and he didn't want to ruin their Christmas by making them concerned for something that was probably just an allergic reaction. Kieran put his t-shirt back on, grabbed his father's cardigan from the reclining chair, covered himself up and went into the dining room to help with the preparations.

Time moved fast on that Christmas Day. The delectable dinner came and went and it almost felt as though they had never even had Christmas dinner.

"I spend all morning fortifying the feast and it's gone in fifteen minutes. Next thing you know it'll be Boxing Day, then the New Year," said Mother as she gathered the plates and cutlery and carried them into the kitchen.

"Come on Kieran you can help me wash up."

The itching persisted throughout dinner, but Kieran had resisted the urge to scratch. It felt like a billion little bugs were scuttling beneath his skin. He took on the duty of washing, which he much preferred than drying the dishes. The soapy water felt soothing against his burning itching hands, but something didn't feel right, one of his fingers felt loose.

"Random question, Mum, but did you place that gingerbread man in my stocking this morning? Father said it wasn't him, but it was a queer looking thing that only he would find funny," said Kieran.

"It most certainly wasn't me, my dear. Guess it must have been Santa," she said, tipping him a wink. They said no more on the matter.

A sharp pain flared in his right hand. Kieran yelped then stifled his mouth.

"Are you all right?" asked Mother. Her one eyebrow was raised in a sign of concern and curiosity.

"Yes I'm fine, Mother, I think I caught my finger on something."

"Well, be careful," she smiled and returned to putting away the crockery.

Kieran lifted his right hand out of the soapy water and what he saw nearly made him spew up his dinner. The middle finger had snapped clean off, tendrils of blood swirled in the sink as he fished out the stray digit, when he found it Kieran wrapped a cloth around his deformed hand and stuffed the severed finger in his pocket.

"Mother I just need to get a plaster. I'll be back," he said.

"Oh honey, I told you to be careful. Do you want me to look at it?"

"No, no, it's fine. I'm fine. Just cut my finger. There's a bit of blood in the sink so you may need to drain it off. I'm sorry."

"You've got nothing to apologise for. Get a plaster and play with Barbara. I'll finish up here."

Kieran smiled, and then ran upstairs to his room in a state of panic.

Chapter Four

He bolted the bedroom door shut and ran into the en-suite bathroom. The reflection staring back at him in the mirror above the sink was a ghoulish effigy. Kieran unwrapped his hand and the cloth was sticky with blood, the wound where his finger had once been throbbed in loathsome pulses. The bleeding had stopped, thankfully, but the congealed crimson cruor smeared over his right hand looked suspicious, like it was some other form of fluid rather than organic plasma. He sniffed the cloth and the smell was spicy and sweet, laden with undertones of copper. Kieran touched the gory remains of the finger stump to his tongue and tasted. It was definitely blood, the metallic aftertaste was too distinctive, but he also tasted cranberries, strawberries, citrus and cinnamon. He could not explain the logic, but his blood was turning into festive jam.

The silent shock was beginning to wear off and the horror of the situation sunk in. Kieran's bedroom was in a more secluded part of the stately home, so he sobbed loud while clutching his marred hand close to his chest. Suddenly his skin crawled with irritation and he scratched his body with rabid frustration. He ripped off his clothes and scratched and scratched and scratched, his body red raw and blistering. The fingernails of his left hand snagged in his chest and the right pectoral peeled from his body, the dead clump of meat landed on the floor with a grisly splat. Kieran's eyes bulged in anguish and he exhaled a horrific scream. Sickly sweet-smelling blood oozed from the gaping hole and beneath the sanguine gash he saw a layer of biscuit. Gingerbread biscuit.

"What is happening to me?" he asked the grotesque reflection in the mirror. His long curly black hair began to fall from his scalp and he ripped out fistfuls of it in hysteria until his skull was completely bald. He heaved and more of that brown vulgar vomit gushed out of him. Lumps of flesh fell from his bones like fat mutated slugs and Kieran saw more gingerbread biscuit beneath the fresh wounds. His tongue flopped out of his mouth; it was a useless dangling muscle that served no more purpose to him. He winced as he grabbed it with his thumb and forefinger and yanked it with force. It tore away with ease and there was no pain. Even though his body was falling apart he felt no more pain, he felt like a reptile shedding its skin. The inside of his mouth became dry, as if he had swallowed sand, and when he licked the roof he tasted gingerbread. The reflection in the mirror was now a foul disembodied spectre of the boy he used to be. The top of his skull cracked and a halo-like ring formed around its circumference. Tears welled in the corners of Kieran's eyes as he reached up and tugged the upper half of his skull away from his head. Underneath he saw the nude gelatinous tissue of his brain exposed to his troubled vision. A layer of gingerbread biscuit began to weave like wicker around his cerebrum until it encased his entire brain. Fresh sobs exploded, and waterfalls of tears cascaded from his eyes until they fell out of their sockets and plopped into the sink. Kieran scrambled blindly for them, but slowly his vision returned and he saw that in place of his organic eyeballs were two obsidian globes of icing.

Something nefarious crept into his mind. He sensed a dark entity feeling around his thoughts, suffocating his rationality and injecting poisonous suggestions into the fabric of his sensibility. He felt hungry, but his appetite was for something unholy, something he would go to hell for if he still possessed a mortal soul, but his essence was being replaced and the malignant metamorphosis was almost complete.

Chapter Five

"Where is that boy?" asked Father. The afternoon was waning and the sun was beginning its early descent in the west. Outside a flurry of snow was being guided by a strong wind that howled through the mansion.

"He said he had cut his finger earlier. Maybe he's napping, dear. He has been through the wars today the poor lamb," said Mother while she added more logs on the fire. Barbara sat by the tree, admiring her presents.

"Shall I check on him?" she said, stroking the hair of a new doll.

"No it's fine, honey, I will," said Father, smiling with loving warmth.

As Jeremy Gascoyne made his way through the winding maze of his home he often questioned why he allowed his son to have a room so far away from their living quarters. It was a question he only asked when he was too lazy to walk the distance.

He stood outside his son's bedroom and knocked the door three times.

"Kieran, are you there, Son?" he called, not wanting to barge in and impose on his son's private time. When he didn't get an answer after the third time,

Jeremy opened the door and walked through. He was surprised the door had not been bolted shut, Kieran was a stickler for bolting his door when he wanted some privacy. The bedroom looked like a walrus had run rampant and ransacked the place.

"Where are you, Son?"

The bathroom door was closed. A feeling of dread touched Jeremy with icy hands. Maybe his son was feeling worse than he had led his mother and father to believe. He tried opening the bathroom door, but it was locked.

"Kieran, open up now. You're starting to worry me!"

No reply. What if he had passed out and hit his head on the bath or the tiled floor? He couldn't afford to be polite anymore and was agitated to the point of desperation. He could, however, afford another door and decided to break this one down. Taking two steps back Jeremy took a moment to gather his strength, he knew it would take some force. He kicked once, nothing. He kicked twice, nothing. He kicked thrice and succeeded. The door gave way and he went sprawling through a pool of viscid gore into a room that looked more like an abattoir than a bathroom. His eyes bulged as the repugnant sights traumatized his mental state. The once polished ivory tiled floor was now painted with streaks of crimson and random pools of blood, and scattered hither and thither were blobs of flesh that he didn't want to accept belonged to his son. It was a room of pure revulsion and he didn't want to be a part of it. Jeremy picked himself up out of the syrupy rouge blood and stepped backwards out of the bathroom. There was no sign of Kieran. The silence was unbearable, Jeremy suffered from tinnitus and in that room the piercing chime sliced through his clarity and filled his heart with severe anxiety. He stepped with caution, eyes hopelessly fixated on the gruesome tapestry of violence in the bathroom. Jeremy felt a presence behind him, but before he could turn around he bumped into something cold and let out a startled scream. It was the metal frame of Kieran's bed. He let out a sigh and laughed nervously. A gust of wind whistled through the room from a wide-open window near the bed.

"For god's sake. I've wasted too much time up here I need..."

A hand shot out from under the bed and grabbed his ankle. Jeremy was yanked to the floor and landed on his back, the hand let go and he scrambled backwards, but before he could get up something started to crawl out of the lifeless void beneath the bed. The wretched creature that appeared from the darkness sent Jeremy's stomach into spasms and he

nearly regurgitated his Christmas dinner but instead was paralysed

completely. All he could do was stare at the monster that had once been his

son. When a dry biscuit hand touched his leg he snapped out of his paralysis

and tried to get away, but the creature was quick and latched on tight.

Jeremy yelled out in terror and the monster slithered out and climbed on

top of him. It was a perverted abnormality made of gingerbread, but Jeremy

knew it was his son.

"Kieran it's me. It's your…"

A malodorous milky white substance belched from the gingerbread man's

mouth and covered Jeremy's face. It smelled of rancid eggnog and burned

like acid. The father shrieked in pain as the acidic eggnog melted the flesh

from his face. The mouth of the monster that had once been his son opened

wide, it unhinged like the jaws of a snake, revealing teeth that looked like

serrated blades, and clamped down on Jeremy's dissolving face.

It ate and did not waste a morsel. But its unholy appetite could not be sated.

Chapter Six

The logs crackled on the fire and the aromas of burning wood and festive spiced candles brought feelings of childhood nostalgia to Martha Gascoyne. The sun was now a distant memory as darkness enveloped the land, signalling the approaching end of another Christmas Day. She always felt melancholy around this hour in the evening. Time had a bad habit of hurtling towards the finishing line before you've had a chance to enjoy the race. Martha was adding the finishing touches to a scarf she had been knitting. It was called it the advent scarf because since December 1st she had been adding to it every day. On it were various festive patterns that represented the exciting build-up to Christmas.

Her husband had been gone for a while and she hoped her son wasn't too poorly; it was such a shame to miss out on Christmas because of an inconvenient illness. When the scarf was complete she smiled and wrapped it around her neck, then got up from the sofa and approached the large window that overlooked the stately gardens. Snow descended upon the land replenishing what had fallen the night before. In the background Martha heard the sounds of A Christmas Carol on the television, which Barbara was watching with avid fascination. She loved the classic Christmas films, just like her mother.

"Barb, honey, would you like some supper? I can make some turkey and stuffing sandwiches," she said.

Barbara's face beamed with delight.

"Oh yes please! But what about Daddy and Kieran?"

"I'm sure they'll be down soon. It's almost time for Father's evening brandy."

When Martha stepped into the kitchen she felt the chill of winter touch her bones, and realised she had not turned the central heating on. She flipped the switch on the boiler and began prepping a satisfying supper for the family. There was nothing that could compare to cold cuts on Christmas night. There were slices of cold turkey, a big bowl of stuffing, cocktail sausages, jars of mustard and cranberry sauce, and turkey dripping to spread on the bread, just like Martha's mother used to do.

The trick is to not use butter, she used to say.

Suddenly there was darkness.

"Mummy the power's gone!" Barbara called from the living room.

"I know, dear, I'll sort it out," replied Martha.

The fuse box was in the attic above the master bedroom and she hated going up there since they had a bat infestation a year ago, but the man of the house was tending to other business. It was up to her to bring light back into their little world.

The attic was originally re-decorated to be a playroom for the children, but they were always too afraid to spend time up there. Over the years it became storage space and housed many artifacts from the mansion's past.

Martha lighted her way using a Victorian kerosene lantern that had been used by Jeremy's grandparents back in the old days. She loved using it during power outages and it made her feel connected to the pas.. There were two Roman columns that flanked the top of the stairs; they looked ominous in the dimness. The wooden floorboards creaked beneath her feet as she walked towards the fuse box. She kept checking for bats, even though she knew they had abdicated long ago. When she lifted the lamp to the fuse box the flickering light illuminated a ghastly scene; the switches appeared to have been melted by some kind of sticky white residue. Martha dared not touch it. All around her the potent fragrance of gingerbread crept inside her nostrils and tickled her senses. Trepidation caused her body to shake with fear. What could have done such an alien thing? In a flash she thought of Barbara being downstairs on her own and turned to rush back to her daughter and stopped dead at the top of the stairs.

It was a monstrosity made of gingerbread, a humanoid creature besmirched with blood and it looked at her with damnable black eyes. It coughed out guttural growls and its mouth twitched like a hungry predatory animal.

"Kieran?" was all she said before the gingerbread man bounced up the stairs with grisly speed. Martha was frozen in place like a snowman on icy ground. She felt a dry biscuit hand wrap around her neck while the other forced open her mouth. Her eyes were swollen with dismay. The flouncing freak opened its mouth and ejected a tremendous tide of white liquid into her mouth, the stuff tasted like foetid eggnog, and it was melting her innards. She tried to scream but no sound could be produced, only a vile gargling that brought excruciating pain. With the last of her life and strength she threw the kerosene lantern at a stack of wooden crates in the corner of the attic, it exploded with orange light and the gingerbread man recoiled. It snarled, opened its mouth wide, lifted Martha up and drank her disintegrating organs through her mouth like it was holding a bottle of Babycham. After it had drunk its fill, the gingerbread man dragged the drained remains of Martha's corpse downstairs away from the blooming fire and fed.

Chapter Seven

Barbara heard thudding upstairs. It was the first thing to draw her attention.

"Mum, is that you?"

The candles that were laid out around the room created oscillating shadows on the walls that made her squirm on the sofa. The second thing to draw her attention was the acrid smell of smoke as she walked up to the master bedroom. Urgency carried her feet swiftly upstairs and she used her phone as a torch to light the way.

"Mum! There's a fire! Mummy!"

Barbara was confused, why was this happening on Christmas Day? Where were her father and Kieran?

The hallway was shrouded in thick smoke and she covered her mouth and nose using a handkerchief from her pyjama pocket. Barbara pushed open the door to the master bedroom and what she saw drove her vulnerable young mind to insanity. The beaming torch emitting from her smart phone emphasised the horror by shining a spotlight on the gore. The mutilated cadaver of her mother lay on the bed and on top of that was a hideous gingerbread demon. It was biting large chunks of flesh from Martha's body and swallowing them greedily. Around its neck Barbara saw her mother's knitted scarf and she finally submitted to screaming. The demonic entity looked at her, under its eyes were frosted teardrops and she recognised it immediately.

"Oh my god. Kieran, what happened to you?"

It gazed at her, fixated on her moistened eyes, then something changed, something evil inside took hold and its face contorted into a vicious snarl. Barbara could not move, her family was dead; her home was burning down, so she closed her eyes and awaited her fate. She awaited her death.

There was an almighty crash as the ceiling collapsed on top of the creature, sheets of flame and clouds of smoke billowed from above. The gingerbread man howled like a werewolf and Barbara seized the opportunity to run, slamming the bedroom door shut behind her in the vein hope of slowing it down. She flew down the stairs praying she would not trip. If she did it would be the end of her. Another howl erupted through the dark house and

Barbara heard the bedroom door shatter, then the thumping footsteps of the approaching gingerbread man. Hiding would do no good, either it would find her or she would burn. Her only chance of survival was going outside and making it to the road, hoping against hope that a car would pick her up and drive her to safety. Hope was all she had left.

Outside the snow continued to fall. What already covered the ground caught the rays of moonlight and reflected them in resplendent twinkles. On a normal night it would be sight to marvel at, something to admire and make one ponder the complexities of nature, but this was no normal night.
The cold almost crippled Barbara with spams, but she stayed strong and slugged it out. She knew the beast was not far behind her, full of hate and hunger. The snow was deep but she was small and light on her feet. The unfinished snowman she and her brother had tried to build earlier that morning stood in front of her. She remembered the fetid brown gruel that had spewed out of Kieran's mouth that morning, and the gingerbread man he ate before breakfast, but there was no time for reflection, first she needed to survive, and then she could piece this eldritch puzzle together.

In her frantic state Barbara ran across the frozen pond, she made it halfway, then the ice cracked beneath her feet and she plunged into the icy water.

Epilogue

A cold and trembling hand burst out of the water and a blue-faced girl emerged swallowing a lungful of air. She felt her heartbeat slowing to a crawl and paddled to the edge of the pond. Barbara hauled herself out while she desperately gasped for more oxygen and fell face first in the snow. Her body shivered violently and each clawing movement was a sluggish struggle filled with savage pain. The snow had ceased its frozen rain and the air was still, but the deadly chill lingered on and for a moment Barbara had forgotten how she had ended up in the pond. There was a flash of lightning inside her head and damaged memories were sewn into brutal images of carnage and distress with gingerbread hands tainting her flesh. She jolted up into a sitting position and that is when the intense heat of the burning mansion hit her, it warmed her face and the incandescent glow almost blinded her. Once her eyes had adjusted, she saw it standing in front of the fire like a statue made of biscuit. It didn't move, it only stared. Barbara scrambled to her feet, the snow which had covered her melted in the heat, leaving her feeling damp and miserable. She stepped backwards with caution, her eyes never leaving the gingerbread man. When she finally felt there was enough distance between them she turned to run for the road before almost immediately stopping dead in her tracks.

Shambling towards the blazing bonfire that used to be Gascoyne Manor were hordes of misshapen gingerbread men. Their mutated biscuit bodies moved with ravenous purpose. Barbara felt her crotch grow warm as her bladder loosened from the sheer terror that coursed through her veins. Something had happened during that Christmas Day, something that reached beyond the walls of her home and spread like parasitic mistletoe across the land. It was a gingerbread holocaust, and only god knew how many had been affected by it. She turned back to face the monster that had once been her brother.

"Merry Christmas, Kieran," she said to it.

The gingerbread man opened its arms and a sinister grin spread across its face and with steady confident steps it crept towards Barbara, for a moment she thought it recognised her and hoped those open arms would greet her with a warm cuddle. A girl could hope on Christmas Day, but instead she closed her eyes and awaited her fate. She awaited her death.

Printed in Great Britain
by Amazon